John Passfield
Saturday Morning

a novel

by

John Passfield

Rock's Mills Press
Oakville, Ontario
2021

Published by
Rock's Mills Press

Cover Design: Craig Passfield

Cover Illustration: A photograph of John and Trudy Passfield, in 1967, with their 1960 Austin Healey Sprite.

Author's Website: www.johnpassfield.ca

Publisher's Website: www.rocksmillspress.com

Chapter 1

Shifting down as we chug up the hill. This old truck likes to take its own time. Like an old horse pulling a wagon and plodding along. She's hauled a lot of garbage in her time. A lot more garbage than I have, that's for sure.

Tales of best sentence and most solas.

Geez – I hope I'm not getting nostalgic. It's a little too early for that. I'm still only twenty-one – going on twenty-two. A little too early to look back fondly over all my years. But it is my last summer – my last month – my last year. The end of what I could call 'my garbage years'.

To be a young man

Collecting garbage on the street.
John and Herm and Fivey.
Building a load in an open truck.

who is starting out

Where do you expect to be fifty years from now?
What do you expect to be fifty years from now?
Do you realize that you'll be older than your parents are now?

on the road of life.

Rows of garbage cans on both sides of the streets.
Waves tumbling onto the beach at a lake.
High school students watching a Hamlet film in the gym.

Making our way up to the streets. Heading for eight o'clock. Should be emptying our first garbage can about ten to eight. A heavy dew last night so our pant-legs will be wet for at least the first hour. Hard to tell how much garbage there's going to be today.

Where ignorant armies clash by night.

Funny how I can remember everything. Everything important anyway. Working with Bumps and Herm and Fivey in the open truck. Working with Frank that summer we collected at all the stores. Working alone out at the car-plant – unloading those rubber-tired train-cars. I've collected ever kind of garbage there could be.

There was a boy who was born to be a hockey star.

"St. Thomas is a small city which is located in Southern Ontario, Canada." "It was founded by Colonel Thomas Talbot in pioneer times."

There was a boy
who was born
inside the globe.

Completely unknown - a faint outline now - scanning the sidewalks - nothing but ink - who tells no story - only a seer could solve - I do my thinking - what good are dreams and nightmares - a lot of heavy work - rusty nails all through the debris.

I think I live life mostly in my mind.
More than the life that people can see.
I live as a full a life as anybody – people can see me in school, or at the beach, or even working on a garbage truck – but there's a lot more of life going on inside this skull.

A moth
will be born
inside a building.

Herm beside me in the truck. Fivey beside him, at the window. Fivey leaning out and looking for people he knows. Always ready to wave a hand and shout hello. He knows everyone in town so he'll soon be shouting. Herm's been silent all the way. Hard to tell what kind of day he's going to have. Don't know whether to have him drive or work at the curb.
I do not think that they will sing to me.
I'd finish my exams every spring at the high school, and then at the university, and I'd be right out on the street. Collecting garbage in wind or rain or sun or hail. The kids in the neighbourhood all envied me. Working forty hours a week. A pretty-good dollar for non-union wages. Better than any of the kids in my neighbourhood could have gotten anywhere else.

There was a boy who was born to be an actor.

Starting out on the first load of the morning.

Oak Street - Elmina Street - Southwick Street - Wilson Street - Gravel Road.

He could see all the people
walking
on the outside of the globe.

Inching along the sidewalk - get inside the words - what's he thinking - of which I know nothing - everything that she treasures - stimulated other questions - wasn't my special pickup - I haven't even started yet - told not to walk alone - skimming the surface of life.

Funny how you can drive a truck, or empty garbage cans, or even build a load and still do other things.

Other mental things that is.

You can even imagine that you're giving an interview.

The writer's problems
spilled over
onto the bookstore shelves.

Scanning the sidewalks as we drive. Doesn't look so bad. Fivey assessing the amount of garbage out at the curbs. So what do you think, Herm? Think we'll get her all off by noon? Could be heavy – could be light. Never tell what you're gonna get when you turn a corner and start a new street.

A thought, to Donne, was an experience.

One more month – or perhaps six weeks – and then I'll be done. No more collecting garbage for me. We're getting married in the chapel. Then off to a two-week honeymoon. It'll be nice to see Quebec City. And nice of my dad to say that we could take his car.

A mother who tells a story of her childhood.
A dad who tells a story of the West.
A grandpa who tells one story of the War.
A grandmother who tells no story at all.

What makes the great books great? Why do the great books achieve greatness while the shallow books remain shallow? How can this be when every one of these books is about the lives that we humans all lead?

I am sitting in the bleachers.
It is the circus in my hometown.
A huge tent in a field by the railway tracks.

I am sitting on the bleachers with my dad.

Do you spend much time thinking of the future?
Do you consider such thoughts a waste of time?
Do you feel that it's best to concentrate on 'the now'?

"Good evening, ladies and gentlemen. Greetings from all of us here at the CBC. Good evening to you all on this day of celebration. It was exactly one hundred years ago today that Canada became an independent nation. And now, for the eleven o'clock evening news."

Do
all birds
sing?

There was a boy who was born on Oak Street.

My day off at Chateau Lake Louise. The other gardeners can do without me for a day. I'm going to hitchhike down to Banff and take the bus back. That way I won't have to worry about getting back on time. Breakfast with the guys before I light out on my own.

A man on the beach collecting driftwood.
A picnic hamper filled with food to the brim.
An old man sitting in a rocking chair.

These moments are the nectar. The hummingbird sips and flies away. Where did the hummingbird go? The flower is brimming with nectar. How soon will the hummingbird return?

Be nice to finish the garbage route by noon. Dump our load and head on home. Nice now, at eight o'clock, but she might be a pretty hot day when we get to noon. Be nice to go to Port Stanley – have a swim and lie on the beach. Take one of the books I'm going to teach and read and think. Try not to get nervous when I think of teaching school.
Much have I travelled in the realms of gold.
Then my new school after Labour Day. It's been a summer of re-reading books. *Hamlet – L'Étranger – Death of a Salesman. Wuthering Heights – Oedipus the King.* And *Gatsby* – and even *1984.* Looks like I'm going to teach all the classics. I was impressed to see the titles on the lists of the courses. But then I took some of the same books in high school. Kids are still kids, after all.

There was a boy who was born to be a garbage man.

So just what, exactly, is a story?

The boy felt odd
to be living his life
inside the globe.

Patterns in the ice - doing a science experiment - a faint outline now - a series of decisions - feel you know yourself - a limit on his skills - each day a thing apart - to impart his wisdom - is there a light - the time is coming.

There are certain things, you understand, that I don't wish to talk about.

My impending marriage, my relationship with my future wife, my future career as a teacher, which – as you realize, I haven't even started yet – and my mom and my dad and my brother and my sister and my relatives.

All of these things I see as my private world.

His strategy
was a little different
than that of most.

Fivey's worked here all his life. A garbage man by choice. There's a rumour that Herm started on the garbage in Toronto, walking behind a horse and a wagon when he was eighteen. Never had the nerve to ask him if that was the case.

I do all that may become a man.

The garbage looks like it might be extra-heavy today. Lots of cans and bags and boxes at every house. But it's always that way when we miss a collection-day for a holiday. I keep thinking that this is Saturday, but on Saturday, we didn't work. This is Wednesday – it's Saturday's garbage that we're collecting now.

There was a boy who was born to be a writer.

Trying to figure out whether the garbage is heavy or light.
Talbot Street - Ross Street - Elm Street - Fairview Ave - Sunset Drive.

The only thing odder
would be
if the globe was inside the boy.

What I think you'll be - you turn a corner - up and down the corridors - been worn by someone else - job that would match - that's just a story - the boy felt odd - for every door there is a key - most interesting drama - a light in the distance.

However, I am willing to talk about my experiences here on the garbage.

After all, it's soon to be coming to an end, so I can't be fired for what I say, and they can't take the money back, and besides, I'm not a vindictive person – I have no axe to grind – so there will be nothing malicious in what I would have to say.

But just to keep things clear – both to me and to you – just what would you say is the purpose of this interview?

The old gypsy woman
was very precise.

Well, I won't be long for this job. Another month or perhaps six weeks. There's the honeymoon and preparation for the new job. A whole new way of life for me from now on.

Full many a glorious morning have I seen.

Hard to believe we're all living in History. History has always been just in the books. The Battle of Hastings – the Plains of Abraham – the Second World War – Waterloo. But Saturday was 'The Centennial of the Country of Canada – A Celebration of One Hundred Years'. No garbage collection on Saturday, but it didn't go away. Now Saturday's garbage – and Wednesday's too – sits out at the curb.

"Old Colonel Talbot's for sure a colourful St. Thomas character."
"No shortage of stories have been told about that man."

A young sapling

Four hours to do the route.
All the garbage must come off.
If there's overtime, you don't get paid at all.

sprouting

What are the things, in the future, that you feel you can control?
What are the things, in the future, that you feel you cannot control?
Do you feel that your ideal future is about to begin?

in a forest.

I started on the garbage when I was fifteen. Walked all day behind a truck. Went home, had some supper and fell into bed. I was a hockey player, but this drew on different muscles in the legs and the arms. Woke up at six o'clock, turned off the alarm and got up and got dressed and back to the job. Still it's only been in the summers. Next summer I'll be going to teachers' college. Doubt if I'll ever feel nostalgic about this job.

Oh Torvald, I've stopped believing in miracles.

So it's quite a big summer for me. End of my education – got my BA at Convocation, last month. The Centennial of my country – one hundred years last Saturday. My last month at twenty-one – I'll soon be twenty-two. Getting married at the end of August. And in September, a whole new career – teaching school. That'll make 1967 a banner year.

Chapter 2

I pull the truck over to the curb. We look along the street and see what there is to see. Garbage cans on both sides of the street stretching to the horizon. Cans on both sides of all the streets in the neighbourhood. But the big question is – is she heavy today?

To be or not to be. That is the question.

I suppose my earliest childhood memory is of the kids all singing that song. I can't remember anything earlier than that. Mom occasionally tells that story of my grandmother admiring my bare bum, at the beach I suppose, and me sitting down on it so she wouldn't be able to see. But that's just a story to me. My earliest memory is of the kids all singing that song.

To be a prince

A little boy who tells the doctor he likes words.
People putting garbage pails out at the curb.
A mouse-catcher in search of a mouse.

who is charged

What is the point of reading all these books?
Are you reading these books instead of living your life?
Are they an excuse to live your life completely alone?

with an onerous task.

The highway to Port Stanley.
A meat market on a busy street.
A subway under the railway tracks.

Riding my tricycle to the end of the street. I was riding it on the sidewalk and then Mom said that the kids will be home soon. I asked her if I could go to meet them. Yes you may, but stay on Oak Street. Those cars come far too fast when they come up that hill. Just wait at the end of the street for the kids to come home.

C'est Vénus tout entière à sa proie attachée.

Colouring pictures in Sunday School. Moses and the Golden Calf. Jesus and the Little Kids. The Sermon on the Mount and the Parting of the Sea. The best is Jacob and His Coat of Many Colours. You can use every colour in the pack.

One day, the whole road froze. Oak Street was one big sheet of ice. His father tied on an old pair of skates. He held himself up with a kitchen chair. His ankles turned in as he tried to stand.

"The Passfield family is actually made up of two families who came to St. Thomas."

"The Passfields and the Davies are families who came to St. Thomas from England years ago."

What was I to do? My husband was dead. I had no one to protect me. Everything I had was predicated on him. Everything I had disappeared when my husband died. I had less security than that washerwoman who does the sheets. I assume that she has a husband and a home. I felt myself to be on the edge of a precipice – looking down at a vast abyss. When I saw a hand reach out, I grabbed ahold.

Avoiding certain thoughts - on high alert - we should be okay - a boat in a raging current - treasured each broken lamp - consider such thoughts - don't live in the same world - stretching the sides of the truck - in on his subtle game - have something to say.

So let's see – how many years has it been? I started after Grade Ten, when I was still fifteen years old. I wasn't old enough to legally drive a truck.

Oh I knew how to drive one, of course – my dad had taught me to drive a car – but I didn't have a licence to drive a truck. But the guys were pretty generous. Some of them let me drive the odd load.

And one guy – it was Bud – always let me drive the middle load – one in the morning and one in the afternoon. He let me drive along the curb and then he would drive the truck back down to the dump.

Half way through the first summer, when I turned sixteen, I passed the licence test, and then I could legally drive.

Say
a dusty old shed
that has not been used
for years.

"The President's body is being flown from Dallas to Washington. A state funeral is being arranged as we speak. There will be a lying-in-state at the Capitol Dome."

Herm and Fivey climb out of the truck while I do my thinking. The garbage doesn't look too heavy today. Some days, after a holiday, it's overwhelming. Saturday and Wednesday collection for the same houses, every week for the summer – so the garbage doesn't set in the cans and stink. Some holidays, people seem to do nothing but generate garbage from their kitchens, from their basements, from their yards. Other holidays – they let the garbage-creation go and take a day off. Today, I'd say the garbage is not too bad.

And midnight hangs the hatchet in the barn.

My job as a newspaper boy, during the winter. The paper boy quit when things got cold and I got the job. I fold the newspapers and deliver them every morning. A bundle is dumped in the entrance of the restaurant at six o'clock. It's cold in the mornings, but Mom always makes sure I dress really warm. I wear an old pair of navy pants that my dad gives me. I wear thick boots with a couple of layers of socks. I wear a couple of sweaters under a greatcoat. It's an old army coat that belonged to my Uncle Ken. Then a toque on my head and a wrap-around scarf. Just my eyes are exposed to the cold. When the route is done, I go home and get ready to go to school.

He grew up watching the movies. An actor was what he wanted to be. Saturday afternoons in the theatres. Playing cowboys and Indians on the way home. Live in Hollywood and have a swimming pool.

Loading a pair of old worn leather suitcases.

Elgin Street - Hemlock Street - Malakoff Street - Pine Street - St. Catherine Street.

That fellow up there on the balcony. All he does is lean and stare. Doesn't seem to want to come down and join the throng. Hops the tram ever morning – hops back down at the end of the day. Never comes in here to buy or to say hello. There's a girl sometimes on the balcony. Doesn't hug her or hold her close. She looks one way and he looks the other. As if the two of them don't live in the same world.

The meaning of the play - how to do it myself - cannot reply to such questions - you'll see his name - heard the cougar growl - all he'd have to do - people all over the world - the books are sinking down - have lost their appeal - caught on a trestle.

The summer after Grade 9, I was in the Militia. Then the next summer I was lucky to get this job. So that means that the summer after Grade 10 – and the summers after Grade 11, 12 and 13 – I worked here, on the garbage.

After first-year university, I went out West to work as a gardener at Chateau Lake Louise, Alberta. Then a summer taking a novels-course and painting my parents' house. Then this summer, I'm back collecting garbage again.

The collecting of the garbage is pretty well the same every day. It's the people you work with who provide the variety, I suppose. There's been a lot of men I have worked with over the years.

There were
intense negotiations
between the words
and the pages.

Waiting at the end of Oak Street. Cars keep coming up Elmina Hill. I am over at the curb in case any of them turn up here. Ann is in Grade One. Bob is in Grade Two. Next year I am going to go to school. But I won't get to take my bike. I'll walk with the other kids. And it's only half a day for the very first year. I think I hear a noise. It sounds like singing. All the big kids from the street are singing a song.

But hush! hark! a deep sound strikes like a rising knell.

Shakespeare is the king of them all. The most talented writer in the history of pen and ink. But what is talent and what is technique? I could never read the plays without reading criticism. What are these critics saying about talent and technique?

A red river running into the heart.
A truck-driver burning out a clutch.
A person who hopes there will be another war.

These critical books that I have been reading lately. Books by Ellis-Fermor, Prior and Clemen. These books are trying to tell me something that I need to know.

The clowns are in the spotlight.
They run and tumble in the ring.
The people laugh and chortle.
A clown is kicked in the pants.

Why should a university student read the great books?
Why should a high-school student read the great books?
Why should anybody bother to read a great book?

"Parliament Hill was the backdrop, today, for a high-profile ceremony, which included the participation of Her Majesty Queen Elizabeth II. The ceremony was well attended by Canadians, who left their homes all across the country in order to be here on this historic day. There were dignitaries on Parliament Hill representing every province and territory and many of the varied peoples who are proud to call Canada their home and native land. There was a feeling of camaraderie as people mingled and chatted and exchanged thoughts about this nation that we all call home. The weather couldn't have been more cooperative, as the sun shone on the Peace Tower on this fair day."

It's just
something
I've wondered
about.

He had a mother and a father, an older brother and an older sister.

I'll hitchhike down to Banff – save my money. See the sights and walk around all day. Take the bus back up to Lake Louise Station. Get the hotel limo there for the ride up the road to the Chateau. All the makings of a really excellent day.

A department store with an elevator.
A bulldozer squashing garbage in a dump.
Free coffee for professionals at a food-bar.

We float boats on the creek behind our house. We push them along with a stick. A slab of wood with a block on top and a pointed bow. Every kid in the neighbourhood has his own. The perfect way to spend a summer afternoon.

"It happened only ten short years ago. The advent of the first artificial Earth satellite – the Russian Sputnik of 1957 – gave to all humankind a new perspective on life down here on the Earth. It was a concrete indication of the tremendous – one might almost say unimaginable – size of the universe – and, at the same time – of the seemingly-unlimited potential of the human adventure."

So what to do with Herm and Fivey? Fivey only has one arm, so it's difficult for him to empty garbage cans. But on the sidewalk, he can grab them with two hands – with one hand and one hook – and lift them off the curb and hand them up. Herm is looking a little unstable – probably had a liquid night. What if he falls and hits his head when the truck hits a pothole or a bone-head driver makes me come down a little sharper on the brake? Better if Herm does the driving – he can crawl along the curb while I build the load.
The sun was like a red wafer – pasted in the sky.

My one-day job selling tickets for service stations. I see a notice in the newspaper. Boys wanted for service-station work. Come over Saturday, early, if you want a job. All week I think how nice it will be. Only a couple of blocks from my home. Pumping gas, cleaning windshields, checking oil.

Actually, he hadn't thought about a full-time career as a garbage man until the time that Frank had spoken – on the last day of the summer. They were driving down to the dump with the final load. And what Frank had said had startled him, as he hadn't thought about it before. Frank looked over at him, as he pumped the clutch and shifted the gears. "Too bad – John – that you're gonna hafta go back to school."

What is a story and what does it do?

I don't know that will become of Hedda. I have nothing to leave her at all. Everything that she treasures in her life will disappear when I'm gone. I don't keep such fine horses on my army pay. And the fancy-dress balls at the officers' mess. They don't invite paupers – dressmakers and governesses and the like – to fancy-dress balls. Better you hadn't been so haughty, Hedda. Better you'd settled for something less. My pert fine lass is riding for a fall.

Sitting in an inner-office - save your boxes - go right through my house - I have to pay - must be near the end - crashing against my chest - strategy was a little different - what the oracle has to say - opened his eyes - not supposed to drive.

There's different kinds of garbage trucks. Some with a crew of two men – some with three. The closed trucks with a bucket – and the one with a great big ram – take a crew of two, and the open trucks take a crew of three.

Don't know what it's like in the winter, but in the summer it's different each day. Every time you go out, you're with a different crew. Guys go and come back from vacation, some disappear for a week or two without a word, and some disappear and never return.

Over the summer – and over the years – you get to know some of the men you work with time and again. Others work on a truck that you don't get assigned to, so you wave to them as they go by on the street, or down at the dump. So you would hardly say that these are people you know.

He would put
the cookies
back in the jar.

The kids are marching along and singing. Almost like they're having a parade. They are swinging their arms and raising their legs off the ground. Now they're waiting for cars on Churchill Crescent. Raggedy-Ann the sailor man! – Ran away with the garbage man! Now they're marching across Elmina Street. Raggedy-Ann the sailor man! – Ran away with the garbage man! Now they're marching up the little hill to Oak Street. Raggedy-Ann the sailor man! – Ran away with the garbage man! My sister's name is Ann. I wonder if they're singing this song about her.

The ceremony of innocence is drowned.

The teacher is tying my shoe laces. So I can go out at recess. She wonders why I don't know how to do it myself. Surely your mother would have taught you by now. You're the only student in the whole of Grade One who needs me to tie their shoes.

He would write a poem about a nightingale outside his window. He would write a poem about some scenes on a Greek vase. He would falter as the tuberculosis invaded his lungs. He would fall in love and be cheated by early death. Cough his lungs out in a room by the Spanish Steps.

Loading the handle and the blade of a broken hoe.

Mondamin Street - Horton Street - Farley Place - Chestnut Street - 5th Avenue.

My dad's mother must have had a difficult life. She was a tough old girl and never had a soft word. She would shout at us kids and chase us out of her field. She was a housemaid in London England, then the two of them ran a greengrocer shop. Came out here to raise a family and her husband died. He went to work one day on the railway and was carried back home. My grandfather died right in front of her eyes, in agony, on the front porch, Dad said. A widow with five young kids and a world-wide Depression to contend with. I never really knew her before she died. She hardly ever spoke to me. Not the kind of person I would be able to talk to now. Too bitter, perhaps, to tell any stories at all.

In some mysterious way - can't even read my watch - the road beneath my shoes - every wish i had - a rift of gold - a boat in the raging current - made up of two families - entirely at home in the air - tells no story at all - solved the riddle.

I've worked with lots of guys in my five or six summers. Old Tommy, I barely knew. I've worked with Frank and Bud and Cliff and Ray.

And Art and Old Doc and Young Doc too. And Herm and Bumps and Fivey and the boss' son.

And guys whose names I could probably remember if I tried – though for many of them, it was just a nickname – not a full first and last name at all.

There's been a lot of men come and go over the years. Sometimes you hear stories about guys who used to work here – sometimes you work with guys about whom you know nothing at all. Like major characters and minor characters – I suppose – in a novel or a play.

"Carry these beans
in your pocket
for thirty years.

"You can see, from this helicopter shot, the defoliant being sprayed onto the trees. It is called Agent Orange and it enables the surveillance crews to observe the enemy movements on the ground. What looks like ants down there are the Vietnamese peasants gathering their families and whatever they can carry and running away."

Every year, when I work on the garbage, I get the idea that I should write an article about how to build a load. How to build a load of garbage in the back of an open truck. I wonder if the *St. Thomas Times-Journal* would be interested.

Oh I am dying Egypt – dying.

My summer in the Militia. The St. Thomas Armouries. Standing at ease in a large hall. The Sergeant-major is giving a talk. When he turns his back, I look around the room. So strange to be in this building. Where my mother spent her teenage years. Her dad – my Grandpa Davies – was the Sergeant of the Mess. She was living here when she met my dad, before the Second World War. I see a door at the end of the hall that probably leads to where they had their apartment. At the back where no cadet is allowed to go. The whole Davies family lived here for a dozen years or more. Guess I'll never get to see where they used to live.

"There wasn't much for the families in England so they left and came out here."

"How the two families got settled in St. Thomas is no longer known."

Water

Old letters buried in bags and boxes.
A race horse trying to find his place.
A garbage truck stuck in a flower-bed.

bubbling up

Why are the great books so little read?
Why do they gather dust on library shelves?
Why do most people shun the greatest books?

from the ground.

I sing the song for my mother after supper. My sister wouldn't tell me what it was. Well, it's a song about a doll. I haven't heard of her for years. Twenty years ago, every child would have that doll. But those are not the original words. I'll try and remember how it goes. So why were they singing the song with those words, I wonder? I'll have to ask Ann when she finishes practicing the piano. Those words don't sound very nice. Kids can be quite cruel. I hope the kids weren't singing of someone that they know.

The lone and level sands stretch far away.

Coming back for my second summer on the garbage. Finding my hourly pay, this year, is a nickel less. Asking the boss why my pay is going down-hill. Should it be less than it was before? Next payday, I find I'm getting a nickel an hour more.

Chapter 3

So we're set and on our way. Inching along the curb and emptying the cans. Tubs and wheelbarrows full of brambles – old paint cans from the basement – rolled up rugs that have lost their usefulness – window-blinds that have lost their appeal. Fivey on the sidewalk hefting can after can, and setting each one – for me – in the side-door. Me in the back of the truck, lifting the cans and turning them over and emptying load after load after load. Herm inching along the sidewalk, stopping at every house on the route. Be a nice day to work when the dew dries up – the bottoms of Fivey's pants are going to get wet. How can anything go wrong with Herm at the wheel?

A good Wif there was of biside Bathe.

I have a name for ever wave. Some days the waves are tiny and some days the waves come crashing against my chest as the water rolls in and sucks the sand from beneath my feet. I have a name for every wave. The biggest waves are 'highberdoozers'. Today, the waves are crashing against my chest.

To be a young man

A workman drinking a pint of chocolate milk.
An old lady wearing very thick makeup.
An old boxer wondering whether it's Hallowe'en.

who is working

Are you prepared to sacrifice for your art?
Are you prepared to forgo the luxuries – and the comforts – of life?
Are you prepared to eke out a living while writing your tomes?

on a garbage truck.

Salt and pepper shakers on a shelf.
A garbage truck creeping along a curb.
An old lady chasing kids out of a field.

I am eighteen years old. My dad is in Toronto for therapy on his arm, from his accident when he fell out of the tree. My mom is waiting for his pay-cheque in the mail. I talk to the man who fixed the steering on our family car. He has heard about my dad and won't let us have the car. When my dad goes to speak to him, on the weekend, he says, Well you know how it is Cyril – you can't really talk to a kid.

For God's sake hold your tongue and let me love.

We took *Hamlet* in Grade 13. I just couldn't figure it out. What was *Hamlet* all about? I remember going uptown and trying to find a library book with some criticism that would help me to sort it all out. Mr. Prior wanted us to write an essay on the meaning of the play. He wanted two pages and I couldn't even write one word. All we did the year before with *Macbeth* was memorize the great speeches. I got ten out of ten on every quiz I wrote. I thought Shakespeare was just a series of memorable lines.

He started playing in the winters on Pinafore Pond. He and his brother would help the kids to shovel the snow. They would play until they couldn't see the puck. The best times were when the ice was clear of snow. You could skate and push the puck for miles and miles.

"St. Thomas has always been known as the railway city."
"It is on a direct railway line between Chicago, Detroit and New York."

I am walking along! On what seems to be a wooden bridge! I carry a satchel of books on my back! Am I delivering them for someone? Are they my own?

What the characters are thinking - paid his tuition - born on oak street - aware of the finer things - about talent and technique - your most disturbing concerns - that prose cannot do - a boy colouring a picture - what am i thinking - if he had lived differently.

What would I have to say? Well, I don't seem to live my life – I seem to absorb. I'm the one in the group who never says a word.

But I notice things that leave the loud ones unaware. Like who has a hole in her sweater and tries to keep it covered up. Like who has some pain in the eyes that the others don't see.

And it will flutter
at a window –
aware
of the grass and the flowers.

Grandpa Davies was a Barnardo Boy. He was sent out here, to Canada, with his brother, at twelve years old. He sent ten dollars of his hundred dollars home to bury his own father. Did he think about this all the time or was it important to him not to think about it at all?

Come live with me and be my love.

That job painting the rooms of a house. My friend, Dennis, gets a painting job. He asks the owner of the house if he'll hire me as well. Dennis tells him that I'm a good worker. Every room in the house will need painting. That's enough rooms to make it, for sure, a two-man job.

He admired the Hollywood stars. Marlon Brando – James Dean – Montgomery Clift. All the agony and the angst of youthful troubles. *On the Waterfront – The Wild Ones – Rebel Without a Cause.* But he came to feel that theirs' were adolescent concerns.

Loading a whole batch of *Ladies Home Journal* magazine.

Gladstone Avenue - Mandeville Road - Pearl Street - Stanley Street - Yarwood Street.

The boards on the bridge light up as I walk on them! Ahead, all is dark! I walk very slowly! I slide each foot ahead and feel for a board! I am only able to move a short distance at a time!

Some pain in the eyes - cedar fenceposts never rot - you seem to have nothing - the variety of life - snap like a bone - such an amazing idea - wants to be someone else - the ability to see herself - will I just sink down - writing your tomes.

That's the kind of life that I tend to live. The kind of life that a person could call 'the quiet life'. The life that I would call 'the life inside the mind'.

The life that people are thinking while they live the life that people see. That's the kind of thing I think about. Presumably that's the kind of thing that I would write.

Even the cover
and the title
could not agree.

My brother and I digging a grave. A man comes over to talk to us. Do you know the play, *Hamlet*?, he asks. I can't believe that I'm talking to a couple of actual grave-makers. I feel as if I'm in a Shakespeare play. We tell him we're not really grave-diggers at all – we're just a couple of kids who are digging a grave. He asks us if we've ever found a skull.

Never send to know for whom the bell tolls.

Hamlet is a young Danish prince. He travels abroad to study at the university, in Wittenburg. His father is the King of Denmark. His father has just won a recent war. He smote the sledded Polak on the ice. Hamlet is born to be a student. He's what you might call 'a natural prince'. He is sensitive and thoughtful. He can play the lute and write an occasional poem.

A person searching for the other half of his soul.
A father teaching his son to sharpen a saw.
A barrel of ink on a table.

There's something that all of my reading is trying to tell me. Something about the books that I would like to write. But all I have, at present, is a very – very – vague idea.

It is dark where I sit on the bleachers.
The spotlight is on the ring.
I feel a movement at my elbow.
There is someone in the dark.

Were your literary heroes very well paid?
Did they make a comfortable living from the sales of their books?
Did they make enough to live a decent life?

"The Passfield family – of Oak Street, St. Thomas, Ontario – consists of five people. The father is Cyril John Passfield. The mother is Gertrude Davies Passfield. The oldest boy is Robert Walter Passfield. The daughter, the middle sibling, is Eltrida Ann Passfield. And the youngest son is John Christopher Passfield."

Do all birds sing --
but some
don't want to?

He grew up and went to Homedale Public School.

"Lake Louise Station closes down at nine o'clock. The last hotel limo leaves at 9:00 p.m. Be sure to be there by nine o'clock. There's a cougar in the area. If you get there late, he'll be looking for a meal."

Church bells ringing on Sunday morning.
A crowd at a baseball game at Pinafore Park.
Rows of bicycles outside a school.

I take piano lessons. Every Tuesday, on my way home from school. Papa

Hayden's dead and gone – but his memory lingers on. When his mood was one of bliss – he wrote jolly tunes like this. I only do this to please my mom and dad.

Boxes of old magazines. Someone used the holiday to clean out their storage room. Don't have time to look at them. Looks like they're all still clean. Some *National Geographic* and some *Newsweek* and some *Time*. Right now I need them for a tail-gate on the back of the truck. I flop the box down where I know it'll do the most good. If I get more boxes like that, I can build a wall.

I have measured out my life with coffee spoons.

That time when I didn't get the job. Sitting in an office in a factory in London. I'm about to become a teacher – I am about to get married – right now, I need a summer job. Been to all the St. Thomas factories to apply and haven't heard back from even one. So now I'm visiting all of the factories in the industrial park in London. The secretary is having me fill out a form. What sort of future do you see yourself as establishing with our firm?

He hadn't answered Frank – he was actually quite surprised – but he fantasized an answer, as they drove between the gates and made their way down the lane of the dump. 'Actually, Frank, I've been speaking to the boss. A frank talk – man to man – over brandy and cigars. And he seems to see a brilliant future for me, as things currently stand. So I'm going to stay on and make the garbage my whole career.'

I never thought about what a story is – or what it does – when I was in elementary school.

I have come to the edge of the bridge! I feel ahead with my foot but I am unable to sense anything but air! Is there a board missing? I lie down and stretch out my arm! Is there another board just beyond the reach of my hand?

No one had left a note - then i knew - all the time in the world - buried under the layers - the thoughts and emotions - have such resonance - sacrifice for your art - intense boiling cauldrons - the only thing odder - could find a novel or two.

Take Cliff, for instance. What is Cliff thinking as he goes about his daily routine? What does he think of his wife and his kids?

What does he think of his job on the garbage trucks? How does he spend his time on the weekends? Does he look forward, Sunday evening, to coming back to work?

His mother marvelled

that the jar
was always full.

Stopping and taking a coffee break. Ten minutes at the most. Stopping along the street at a little store. The coffee is blistering in these cups. Barely hold it in your hand. Set it on the dashboard until it cools off. I'm the only one who ever takes a rag and dips it in water, and washes the dozens of coffee-rings from the dash.

He was not of an age, but for all time.

But Hamlet's life is changed abruptly. An urgent message calls him home. Something is happening in the castle. His father has fallen asleep in his orchard and not woken up. There is a massive state funeral, but no sooner have the mourners shed their black robes than another court occasion takes place as well. Hamlet's uncle becomes the new king. There is much confusion as to how it has all come about. And the king's new bride turns out to be Gertrude, Hamlet's mom. All of this is disturbing to Hamlet, but he holds his tongue.

He would be wounded in the First World War. He would write short stories in Paris in the out-door cafés. He would go to the bull-fights and write a roman à clef. He would write a novella about an old man and some sharks. Take a shot-gun one day and turn it on himself.

Loading a batch of old letters tied with a string.
Scott Street - Metcalfe Street - Inkerman Street - Dunkirk Drive - Alma Street.

"John is a pleasant little boy. He is very quiet and barely answers when spoken to. Nevertheless, he is always polite and well-mannered. I sense that he would like to make friends, but is unsure as to how to go about it. He enjoys being near the other children, but tends to play alone. I am sure that he will be fine as time goes on."

The only one who worries - the lives that we humans all lead - place the pen on the paper - what am i thinking - a very interesting life - haven't earned a dime - i grabbed ahold - walk home under the streetlights - a long long road - an ordinary life.

Cliff was a married man with kids. It was almost quitting time at Saturday noon. The boss was fit to be tied. – "Who dumped this grain on the floor? – You never dump grain on a concrete floor!" The boss's son had dumped the grain because he needed the truck.

So three of us were set to shovel the grain into the back of another truck, to save the grain from rotting on the concrete floor. There was Cliff, the married man with children, and we two college kids – Young Doc and I. As soon as the boss rounded the corner, Cliff was in his car and was gone – the two of us stayed and shovelled for two hours with no prospect of a cent in pay after quitting time.

But the next payday – to our surprise – there was a ten-dollar bill in our pay envelopes and a one-line note of thank-you from the boss. Young Doc had a ten-dollar bill and so did I. Neither one of us ever asked Cliff – I guess we didn't want to know – did Cliff leave early and still get a ten-dollar bill?

"Nurture these beans
in the soil
for twenty more.

The article would take the reader through the steps of building a load. The floor and the sides of the truck – the types of garbage that people put out at the curb. How you bring the two together – the garbage and the truck – by knowing how you go about building a load.

They also serve who only stand and wait.

My one-day taxi job. The garbage isn't hiring. All of last summer's guys are coming back this year. I should never have quit working there. Now I need a summer job. I start to work as a teacher in September. I won't get paid 'til October the first. The taxi owner gives me a lecture – about how the busses are subsidized while the taxis are not.

"There have been dozens of railway stories in St. Thomas over the years."
"Someday maybe someone will want to write them down."

A bottle

A person building a load in a garbage truck.
A person who has never tasted Chinese food.
A person waiting for a circus to start.

of ink

Would you say that a teacher in Ontario is quite well paid?
Won't you be so busy with teaching that you won't have time to write?
Haven't you chosen a life that will leave no time for your art?

on a desk.

Wonder how Bumps is holding up these days? Didn't see him down at the yard. Bumps must be on a two-man truck with Bud. Bud's a really good guy – he lets the other guys drive – the guys who shouldn't really drive – but Bumps can't drive at all. Don't know why – maybe he's never had a licence –

but when I started on the garbage, neither did I. It's just that some guys never drive – and Bumps is one of them. I suppose it's because of the seizures. Even at one mile an hour, he could still do harm. Don't know when I first realized that Bumps doesn't drive.

He trusted to have equalled the most high.

And then one night, something mysterious appears on the castle wall. The night is cold and blustery – with crashing waves. The news is brought to Young Hamlet – he shares his late-father's name. And he finds himself standing on guard – with a trusted friend or two – waiting for a ghost to appear and tell him the news. Suddenly – there it is! The ghost of Hamlet's father! The ghost has something that he wants Hamlet to do. The ghost speaks above the sound of the crashing waves. And what he says throws a wrench into Hamlet's plans.

Chapter 4

Here we are at Colonel Bramble's house. Been here many times before. He always has a wheelbarrow with a load of brambles, tied three times around with twine, and with a pitch-fork leaning against the side. He always meets us at the curb and, as we pitch the brambles on, he asks the same question that he always asks: how goes the battle, boys? And we always say not bad – not bad at all. Then we move along the curb and he puts the pitch-fork in the wheelbarrow and wheels it away. I never ask him where he gets so many brambles. He seems to have a new supply almost every week.

One truth is clear: whatever is is right.

I suppose my childhood ended the day I started Kindergarten. No more waiting for the kids to come home from school. No more listening to Miss Scarlet on the radio and helping Mom hoe the weeds in the garden and watching her seal the jars of raspberry jam. But the last day of my childhood is not a memory to me. Most of the changes in one's life go unobserved. It would have been Labour Day, of course. We probably spent it at Uncle Claude's cottage at the beach.

To be a young man

A taxi driver trying to collect his fare.
A boy who wants to read all the great books in the world.
A prospective-teacher who knows how to drive a truck.

who loves a girl

When you read – do you get depressed?
What life did Oedipus get to live?
A cartoon character – run over by a steam-roller – lying flat on the road?

in a white roadster.

A couple of swimmers lying on a raft.

An old man making a joke about a dog.
A brick road with an unused trolley track.

Cold and wet down here in Port Stanley. It's early in the spring. Glad I got my jacket on. Walking along the road above the cottage. My dad came down to check the water pipes to see what needs to be fixed before the season. Uncle Claude is checking his cottage too. We brought a lunch but it was too cold to eat on the beach. The wind was blowing and it was whipping up the waves. Bob and Ann are down on the beach collecting drift-wood. Told Mom I wouldn't be too long. Blacky and me climbed the hill. He's my dog so he always comes with me. Blacky never seems to get tired. I have to stop and catch my breath. Took me a long time to climb up the hill. I was huffing and puffing when I finally reached the old road. Walking along and looking at all these old cottages up on the hill.

What oft was thought but ne'er so well expressed.

My first day of kindergarten. What must that have been like? Miss Canning welcoming us to our new home – our home away from home. Lying on a towel to take a nap. Drawing with coloured crayons on a piece of heavy brown paper. I drew my house on Oak Street with the oak tree in front. Was that the day of that terrible windstorm? It was all I could do to hold my drawing on the way home.

He played hockey at the local arena. A better skater than some of the rest. He had taken a year of figure-skating with his sister and her friends. House League Peewee and Bantam and Midget. He won championships and scored his share of goals.

"The Passfield grandfather, Robert Edward, was a carpenter by trade."
"He got a job on the railway soon after he came to St. Thomas."

A bond-salesman. A successful bond-salesman. That's what I want to be. That's climbing the heights for a boy who comes from where I come from. Serve the customer – serve the company – serve me. A gin and tonic at the end of a satisfying day. Boy I sure was lucky to get to live in this house. I got a tremendous break on the rent. I have no idea who lives in that palace across the way.

Some of the stories - serve to buoy you up - like a fisherman in a storm - the circus played here - there were intense negotiations - there are certain things - captures the rituals - you can't possibly know - and not find one - looked incredibly bright.

They say you should write about what you know. Oh I could write about my family, but how would I do that? And what if they didn't like it, then where would I be?

My dad almost died one time. He was working on cutting a tree, and the tree shifted while he was on the ladder and he fell and punctured his lung and it filled with blood. He spent months recuperating with therapy, and in some ways – for physical labour – he has never been the same.

My mom used to take me when she visited her mother. It was cancer and it was just a matter of time. My mom has sometimes said – I've heard her say from time to time – that she fears that the same will happen to her.

The window-sill
will be covered
with the bodies
of the moths
of many years.

"The President's widow, as you can see, is leaving the plane. You can see that her clothing has a number of dark stains. Needless to say, these stains were caused by the President's blood."

I asked Dad, one time, how it felt have his own dad die when he was seven years old. He said it never affected him at all. He just went on with life as if nothing had happened. I never mentioned it again. Neither did he. I wonder if he talks about it with Mom.

Look on my works, ye mighty, and despair!

My job as a newspaper boy, during the winter. I deliver the newspapers to the doorsteps. Once a week, I go around and collect the fee. On Saturdays, I make the rounds and collect the money. Some people pay the *London Free Press* for six months or a year. Most people pay by the week and give the money to me. Once a week, I ride my bike uptown, and pay at the office. I get a percentage of every paper on the route. For every week the homeowner pays, I give him a ticket. The Saturday-paper-only is a separate fee.

Actually, what appealed to him most was the classical actors. Shakespeare was lost to the actors in Hollywood. They could act in entertainment, but not in literature. Skimming the surface of life with not a thought of its depths. They would sound silly when reading the words from a poetry book.

Loading a stack of old yellowed newspapers.

Kains Street - Mary Street - Omemee Street - Walnut Street - Alexandria Avenue.

The old guy brought his kids in here. They're as full of it as he is. He was still babbling in the toilet when they left. I seen it all before – I seen it many and many a time. A rotten tree produces rotten fruit. You don't get kumquats from an avocado tree. You make a kid – you make yourself. You puke in your bed – you gotta lie there. Just lemme close up the place and I'll go home.

A short distance at a time - the blank patches on the map - who is blinded - located in the heart - on the world stage - not too terribly bad - love to scan the landscape - never had a taste - showed what he could do - couldn't see the puck.

My brother got hit by a train. He and some friends were caught on a trestle, and he lay down and the train went over him and the cow-catcher caught his back-pack and scraped his back. And I remember him lying there in the hospital in a white hospital gown and the nurses having emergencies out in the hall.

My sister had scarlet fever. My parents seemed to feel that it was pretty severe. I was just a little boy, and I don't know how dangerous it was, but I remember that I was afraid she was going to die.

My sister and I took our grandpa – Walter Davies – to the hospital – this was only last year. He insisted that my sister should drive, because she was more gentle with the car. All three of us seemed to know that he wasn't going to come out of the hospital alive.

*Each felt
that he deserved
the final say.*

All the old cottages along the road. They are all much older than ours. Mom told me they were built here a long time ago. Most of them have boards on the windows. Some have padlocks on the doors. They are all built on the hillside. Each little sidewalk is like a bridge over a moat. They have turrets and angle-bay windows. Mom said each one has a 'widow's walk'. In the old days, people could look out over the lake and see the boats. I better turn around and go back. I don't know how long we've been away. Almost forgot about the others. Blacky! C'mon! We don't want to be left behind! Mom told me not to be long! Uncle Claude told Mom he has to get back to town! We walk back along the road and then start back down.

We murder to dissect.

Oedipus the King is the most perfect work of literary art. Every concept about life itself is in that play. But it doesn't have the variety of life that Chaucer and Shakespeare have. It doesn't have the spice of the everyday. And yet it contains everything I would want to say.

*A daughter trying to wake her father on a lawn.
A boy who buys a defective sports car.
A worker perched high on a load of trash.*

So not one of the great books is completely realistic. This is Ellis-Fermor's main point. She gives examples of how each book conveys more than just a plot.

A lady stands beside me.
It is hard to see in the dark.
I turn and look at her for a while.
My eyes begin to adjust.

What value is reading about Willie and Biff to students in high school?
Why would they want to see those people in themselves?
What kind of future for these students does that promise to be?

"St. Thomas, Ontario, Canada is a town which was typical of every town in Canada today. It is a city which is located in the heart of South-western Ontario, about half way between Detroit and Buffalo. It is as Canadian as any town could possibly be. It has taken part in the celebration of this great land of ours for the past year. Today, the people of St. Thomas did themselves proud."

Do all birds sing –
but some
are not allowed to?

He played hockey in winter and baseball in the summer.

Hitch-hiking down to Banff. So happy to get a ride. Nice of the heating-guy to stop and pick me up. Enjoying the mountains on either side as we ride and chat. "Them cougars don't take no prisoners – I'll tell you that."

A dinner of fish and chips for thirty cents.
A man with poor brakes on his car.
Garbage cans waiting at the curb.

I join a neighbourhood band with my sister. I tell them I'd like to play the drums. They don't need any more drummers. They give me a mouthpiece and tell me to blow. That's the first step in learning to play the horn. My cheeks puff up, my face goes red and I almost faint. Everyone thinks there must be an elephant in the room.

"It was not so long ago, ladies and gentlemen. Certainly within a living lifetime, when turn-of-the century fantasists were speculating about the possibility of human flight within the 20th Century, and wondering whether it would ever come to pass. And now, in sixty-seven short years, our possibility-horizons have expanded to the very realistic assumption that humankind will one day set foot on the Moon."

Well, I'd like to be a writer. That's what I'd like to be above all. I like to look along the rows of shiny paperbacks. The great titles all in a row – *The Iliad – The Odyssey* – all the Shakespeares on the shelf. *Howard's End – Heart of Darkness – Middlemarch – Bleak House.* I'd go to the bookstore every Friday. Browse the great titles and buy the odd one. All the great authors arranged alphabetically. Some day I'd like to have my name on some of those books.

Give me the ocular proof.

My one-day job selling tickets for service stations. I'm sending a car-load of boys to Chatham. Just a short distance down the 401. There's a gas station under new management. Expect the tickets to sell quite fast. People will snap them up when you tell them what they will gain. For every ten-dollar ticket you sell, there will be a dollar for you. Sell one ticket at every household – all the way up and down the block – and you're going to need a sack to carry your dough.

And so he imagined himself as having a full-time career as a garbage man. What it would be like to make the garbage his full-time career. Up until now, he had only worked at collecting garbage in the summer. He only did it because it paid better than most other jobs. But as time when on, he would come – no doubt – to see it as a craft.

I never thought about what a story is or what it does when I was in high school.

Hamlet is looking into things much too deeply for my taste. I believe that my Lord Hamlet is tempting the fates. He seems to feel that his making of jibes at the new king's situation will be allowed to continue apace. But perhaps he should consider that the new king might want to secure – by a bold and unexpected action – a more stable throne. Well might My Lord talk of mighty opposites, but at this juncture, my advice is to make pause in order to consider what those mighty opposites might now be. Might the new king's ambition and his current situation be the hammer and the anvil of the two? And who – my dear Prince Hamlet – my boy-hood and school-hood friend – might be the nut that is poised for the king to crack?

As the manual said to do - you had no idea - are they my own - that people would assume - all his goals - defies both time and death - a boy they don't know - never in the cards - it didn't go away - what might be their thoughts.

Every family in the world is the same. They have the same hopes and fears. The same terrible feeling that life has terrible things in store.

I was crawling under the ground. We kids had dug some tunnels in the yard next door and you could wriggle – with a lighted candle – from hole to hole. At any time, I could have been buried if the tunnel had collapsed.

My wife-to-be and I almost died together. We were driving in our car. And the brake-pedal suddenly went down flat on the floor.

The mother
was thinking about
the jar and
the boy and
the cookies.

Blacky and me start down the hillside above our cottage. It's hard to move very fast. There's weeds and mud on the hillside. I have to pick my way. I'm about half-way down when I get a shock. Our car is moving down below us! Slowly moving along the road! It looks like a small black beetle! It's gradually moving away! It's way down below me! It's a million miles below! Why would everyone leave without me? They all knew I went for a walk! I'll never get there in time to stop them! They're all going back to town! I try to move faster down the hill, but I trip and fall! I get up and scramble some more but it's muddy and full of weeds! I shout out loud for them to stop! All I can see is the roof of the car! I shout and shout but they don't seem to hear me! The car keeps moving along the road! A black beetle moving across the sand! It moves underneath a tree and then it's gone!

He was a verray, parfit, gentil knight.

The teacher is standing behind my desk. I don't breathe while he is standing there. I don't move my pen. One of the boys shouted 'Norm!' in the schoolyard. I was in the same group as the boy. I hope he doesn't ask me who it was.

He would be handsome and always walk with a limp. Traipse around Europe and write a poem that would make him famous overnight. He would be mad, bad and dangerous to know. He would shake the dust of England from his feet. He would fight for independence in the swamps of Greece.

Loading a taped shopping bag with a note that says 'TRASH'.

Princess Avenue - Myrtle Street - Hiawatha Street - Chester Street - Wilson Avenue.

My other grandma – Grandma Davies – might have had a good life. Until she got breast-cancer near the end. My mom sometimes worries that she will get it too. A young girl in Faversham England. Fell in love with a sailor-lad. Married and had five kids. Picked hops as the kettle boiled while her kids played games in the fields. My mom makes life at the Mill House sound like a dream. But her mother must have worried about her husband – away at the war. A little old lady with snow-white hair in a dressing gown. I was only five years old. My mom and I used to visit her until she died.

The icy stream - who was born to be - if something comes up - there was no change - like a fisherman in a storm - it's overwhelming - an erudite analysis - fill each one with something - do you reach perfection - how you build a load.

All of these events are very clear to me. I think about such things, in one way or another, nearly every day. But what would be the point in writing about my family?

These things happened. They're very real. All of these people in my family were in danger and some of them died.

But it's all just bits and pieces. What you could call 'images of experience', I suppose. But how would I make a book out of memories like these?

*"The beans
will be active
underground.*

"The internal politics on the allied side of this war in Vietnam have taken many twists and turns. It is to be hoped that a much more stable government for a democratic Vietnam is now in place. If so, it can mean a much more vigorous and productive conduct of the war."

I wonder if the *Times-Journal* would be interested in my article. It would be a little different than what they usually do. Not news – not sports – not entertainment. Just an article on how you build a load.

Things fall apart; the centre cannot hold.

My summer in the Militia. The St. Thomas Armouries. We sit in a briefing room. The Sergeant-major is giving a talk. First, your skin will turn blue. Then, your hair will start to fall out. Then, your vital functions will begin to shut down. Then your skin will start to melt and fall off the bone. We sit at the tables, in the briefing room, with our pencils and our notebooks, and write it all down.

"Robert Edward Passfield was killed in a railway accident."
"He left a widow and five young children behind when he died."

A caterpillar

A boy sitting at a piano and refusing to play.
A play that is not entirely realistic.
A book and a towel and some sand.

metamorphosing

So literature is about the crushing of hopes and dreams?
About the withering of the flower as the day moves on?
Why show a high-school student what life is all about?

in a cocoon.

Jumping down onto the road! Almost falling on my face! The sand is hard on the road and I twist my foot! Getting up and starting to run! Blacky is running at my side! We'll never catch up to the car! What is that up at the corner? It's our car! – they're coming back! Why did they drive away without me? I told them I was going for a walk! I told them I would be gone for just a while! Why did they drive away and leave me on my own? The car is slowly moving along! – creeping like a black snail! You can break a spring on this sand, my dad always says! It has to be! – it has to be our car! – I wave my arms as I run towards them so they'll know it's me!

And I blessed them unaware.

Giving a ride to a man on the highway. Wondering why he is asking these questions. Is there a light where you say we're gonna part? Will there be any other people around? Is he planning to shoot me or stab me? Take my wallet and my car? Do I tell him that neither one would be worth his while?

Chapter 5

Nine o'clock already and I'd say were okay on the route. Not bad timing for what we seem to have today – not too terribly bad at all. The garbage is pretty heavy today, but that's typical for the first day on a route after a holiday. Not too heavy if you think of it as Saturday's and Wednesday's garbage combined. No – I'd have to say it's not too bad at all. I'd also say that we're working our way to a pretty full load. There's always a point where you can't put much more on without stretching the sides of the truck. So – let's keep on going 'til nine-thirty – then to the dump and back. Then we can start the second load about ten o'clock. If it keeps up like this – if it doesn't get any heavier – we won't have to work any overtime.

Life like a dome of many coloured glass.

Lying in bed in the summer evenings. Listening to the marching band. The regimental band of the Elgin Regiment at the Armouries. Falling asleep to marching tunes. A gentle breeze coming in through the window-screen.

To be a young man

A workman wrapping a chain around some timbers.
A student writing a humorous essay for class.
A family living in an armouries.

who is reading

Why would certain topics be off-limits in your thoughts?
Why are there things that you don't want to think about?
Is this a case of avoiding your most disturbing concerns?

the greatest books.

A Sunday School Picnic in the park.
Elementary students playing at recess.
Fireworks bursting in the sky.

We are in Trigonometry class. The news comes over the speaker that President Kennedy has been shot. It is not clear, at this time, if he will live. Sitting in stunned disbelief. Trigonometry on the page. Not a sound as we sit and stare. The world is on fire and the brain is numb. This is our atomic-bomb. Sitting and waiting for the bell so we can go home.

There was a sound of revelry by night.

L'Étranger should be a beautiful book to teach. The kids were discussing it when I sat at the back of the class. They were fascinated by the fact that Meursault never explains his thoughts. The teacher said it never fails. Just ask the kids what they think. Don't tell them what to think. You just point out the facts. Leave the meaning to the kids. Just keep opening up new avenues to explore.

He was invited to play on the All-star Team. They played against other cities. He was good, but he wasn't one of the best. Still, he went up and down his wing as the coach asked him to do. He got his picture in the paper when he scored a goal.

"St. Thomas is the site of the demise of the world's greatest entertainment superstar."

"Jumbo died in a railway accident when the circus played here in 1885."

I am a race horse! Somehow, I know that I am a race horse! I can run as fast as the wind! I am not at home as I trot around this farmer's field! I will run as fast as I can and jump the fence!

What the characters are thinking - all of these things - chase the puck - never touch any dials - something i've wondered about - a new-born moth - time will have passed - something i'm keeping in wait - have a thought - all I have to do.

So what's all this about parallel lives?
What is the point of 'the dyer's hand'?
If water can so easily be displaced, can humans too?

And the new-born moth
will be fluttering out its life –
aware, only by instinct –
purely by instinct –
of the flowers
and the grass
and the trees.

Mom told us about the peanut butter. How their dad left the train and brought peanut butter back to eat. It's Canadian, he said. You spread it on the bread with a knife. Always with Mom, a happy memory. Does Mom have any sad memories at all? Well – her mom dying of cancer would have to be one.

A sadder and a wiser man.

That job painting the rooms of a house. Dennis is on the ladder painting the curlicues in the ceiling. Dennis puts me to work painting the window-frames. The man climbs the stairs and says hello and starts to talk about the curlicues. How he wants the ceilings to be painted. I stop painting and stand by the ladder and listen to instructions, so I'll know how he wants the ceilings to be done. The man leaves and we go on with our work.

The boy thought that he would like to be a classical actor. I wish I had a voice like some of those thespians that I have heard. They make the words leap right up off the page. Better than I could ever imagine them sounding myself. Though a Canadian accent probably wouldn't go over too well.

Wondering when to go down to the dump with our first load.

Dieppe Drive - Fingal Road - Hincks Street - Woodworth Avenue - Redan Street.

I am running from meadow to meadow! Somehow I know that I am a race horse! I am not a wild stallion to chase the wandering breeze! I am not at home on the side of this mountain! I will run as fast as I can towards the town!

Born to be a student - nowhere to put it - like to be a writer - invited to immerse - bubbles blown by the gods - certain topic to be off-limits - could see the fireworks - only a tiny dim light - people have a container - i seem to absorb.

What we are or what we do?
What we are given or how we respond?
How many years has Old Tommy spent in the back of a truck?

The reader
finally turned
and walked away.

I am twenty-one years old. Every night the news includes a body-count. A straight line from Buffalo to Detroit would go right through my house. I am a Canadian citizen. If I were American, I would be sent to Vietnam.

Betwixt damnation and impassioned clay.

Meursault is a young Algerian. Algeria is a colony of France. Meursault has a job in an office. He has a balcony on his apartment. He watches people strolling up and down the street. He likes to go to the beach. He likes to swim and go to the movies. He has a girl-friend named Marie. Day after day his life is pretty-much the same.

A boy holding horses outside a theatre.
A person who answers a riddle and saves a town.
A lady riding a horse that she cannot afford to buy.

That Shakespeare was born a poet, but taught himself how to write his plays. This seems to be Clemen's central point. Shakespeare wrote at least twenty of his plays before he knew.

It is a lady dressed in spangles.
She is waiting in the aisle.
In the aisle between the bleachers.
She is waiting for her turn.

Don't you feel that life should be faced, fully and squarely?
That life should be a series of decisions, consciously made?
A bulldozer, making a straight and determined path?

"The Passfield family arose early this morning – Saturday, July 1, 1967 – eager to enjoy this gorgeous day. Then they – or at least the mother, Gertrude – packed a picnic lunch. For supper, there would be hotdogs on the beach. The rest of the family gathered their bathing suits and towels and other beach paraphernalia. Then, when they were ready, they all got in the family car and drove to Port Stanley. Their Uncle Claude has a cottage on the beach."

Do all birds sing --
but some of their voices
are crude and harsh?

The family spent a lot of time at the beach.

"Gotta be back at the boilers by this afternoon. Too bad or I woulda given you a ride. If you hitch-hike, you won't have to pay for a bus. Enjoy your day in Banff – there's a lot to see in a day. The shift I'm on starts sharp at four o'clock."

A young man putting air in a tire.
An old man and his grand-kids out for a walk.
A young man and his friend riding the rails.

I man the hose for my first fire in the dump. The guys on the other hose sweep along and drench my hat and my clothes. Hard to tell if they're having fun at my expense. I wait a while and then I drench them back. Later, I tell the boss that I'm still not used to the hose.

I've been reading some of those writing-manuals. They all say 'Write about what you know'. So – what do I know? Well – I know a lot of the great classic books of literature. And I plan to read a whole lot more. So – should I write about Macbeth? – about Cathy and Heathcliff? Or should I write about going to the cottage and taking a walk with my dog? How do writers come to know what it is that they know?

There was a roaring in the wind all night.

That time when I didn't get the job. Sitting in an outer-office in a factory in London. Two people in an inner-office chatting about the vacations that they have had. About the vacations they might or might not take this year. Two people who seem to have all the time in the world. I hoped to cover a number of factories. I have their addresses and my route all mapped out. One of these two chatter-boxes is supposed to interview me for a job. How many hours are these two going to talk like this?

The winters would be crisp and cold. The sun would sparkle on the snow. His breath would be a white cloud as he walked along the streets. The chains would jingle on the tires of the cars. He would be thankful that he was getting to spend his days out of doors.

Nor did any of my teachers ever talk about what a story is and what it does.

I am running along the city streets! Somehow I know that I am a race horse! I am not one to pull a wagon of bread or of milk! I am looking for a race course! I need to run between the lines with thundering hooves!

Put an image at the end - work with eyes open - was told in dispatches - what she'll look like - his warning saves the boat - reluctance to apply himself - the life inside - stage on which he could stand - no shortage of stories - move back a step or two.

Old Tommy retired in about my second summer. Everyone called it 'Tommy's Retirement Year'. He would come to work with a uniform all pressed and clean.

And he would work for eight hours in the back of a truck, emptying every kind of thing that came out of a can. And at the end of the eight-hour shift, he would be neat and clean as a pin. Not a hint that he'd been handling garbage all day.

The boy
was thinking

of something else.

Piles and piles and piles of garbage. An old sleigh with the paint all faded. The runners are covered in rust. Sitting out in the July sun for one last ride. Hand her up here, Fivey – I've got the perfect spot.

If winter comes, can spring be far behind?

Meursault's old mother is in a home. It's quite a long way from Algiers. Meurault goes and visits her once in a while. Then one day, the old mother dies. He goes to sit with her body at the wake. For some reason unknown to us, he sheds no tears. So what's he thinking as he sits there at the funeral? Is there any hint anywhere else in the book? How do we know what someone is thinking if they never say?

He would write poems that people would assume were translations from the Welsh. Have a magnificent voice and chant like an ancient bard. He would write images that no one could understand. He would go sodden as lesser men bought him drinks. As he died, he would think of the men who were singing at home.

Deciding to take our first load down to the dump.

Locust Street - Pearl Street - Curtis Street - Palm Street - Churchill Crescent.

"John is what I would call an average student. He works diligently at what he finds interesting, but he allows his attention to wander and sometimes neglects to apply himself to the task at hand. Nevertheless, he is always cooperative and obedient and his comportment leaves nothing to be desired."

Where is it now - my private world - this could be the moment - sounds like singing - discern a distinct personality - the garbage-creation - know that winston feels - heart could not be burned - what's around the corner - have all been pioneers.

Old Tommy's wife was a white-haired little old lady. She used to be waiting for him, every time, on the porch. Wave to her husband as he went by in the garbage truck.

The day before Tommy turned sixty-five was his very last day on the job. Neat as a pin when he came to work – neat as a pin at five o'clock. Looked as if he'd never spent a day on the job.

"At the end
of the fifty years,
some flowers will grow."

My dad was quite hurt when the newspaper turned down his article on Florida – all the sights that a typical tourist sees. Told him that everyone goes to Florida – told him his article wasn't really news. He still has his article from 1928 – a whole column in the *Times-Journal*. It was news when hardly anyone went there at all.

For he on honeydew hath fed.

My one-day taxi job. Sitting and waiting in the taxi office. The taxis are on the lot. The driver next to me on the bench turns and talks. I don't yike fyoot, he says. He smiles and his teeth are like a graveyard. Sorry, I say, I don't quite know what you mean. Some of the stones in the graveyard are broken and worn. I don't yike fyoot, he says, but I can't tell what he wants to tell me. His skin is pasty and he constantly blinks his eyes. Many of the grave-stones are missing. He looks at me and repeats himself, getting louder and louder each time: I don't yike fyoot! – I don't yike fyoot! – I don't! yike! fyoot!

"The Jumbo story was told in dispatches from St. Thomas to New York."
"It's a St. Thomas story that is recorded in the *New York Times*."

A couple of beans

A stage on which a person could stand.
A garbage man out for a leisurely stroll.
Questions that are as bothersome as flies.

in a pocket

Are you just a daydreaming, would-be-writer?
Floating in a bubble above all the bushes with prickly thorns?
Ignoring the light above the exit-door of your dreams?

for thirty years.

Well, I'd have to say that this is a full-enough load. 9:30 already, but we're making pretty good time. Better to go down to the dump now and then start in again. I climb down to the street and Herm shifts over on the seat and I slide in behind the wheel. Fivey slides in beside Herm. Fivey always likes to sit at the window, as he likes to call out to everyone he knows. He always leans out the window and waves. Hey Shifty! – or Hey Nifty! – or Hey Swifty! – wouldn't a tall cool one go good right about now? We don't say much as we make our way down to the dump. You know – she ain't so bad today. I wouldn't wanna bet against gettin' her done on time.

I gave commands; then all smiles stopped together.

Meursault is easy to get along with. He falls in with a man named Ramon. Ramon invites Meursault to come to the beach. They have a run-in with a man who challenges Ramon. Meursault ends up with a gun. Strange things happen to us sometimes. He ends up with a gun in his hand and the man who has challenged Ramon in front of his eyes. The man is coming towards him – the sun is hurting Meursault's eyes. What would you do in this situation if Meursault were you?

Chapter 6

Back up on the streets. In and out of the dump in pretty-good time. Can't race across the dump 'cause we'd break an axle. I was warned about that when I first started to drive and I've never forgotten. The dump seems like a great big mattress. Load after load of compacted garbage with soil and gravel on top. If the springs get bouncing, you can snap one like a bone. With the truck out of commission, the boss would probably send us home. Then one less crew of guys would be working overtime – without any pay.

The course of true love never did run smooth.

Stealing clover from my grandma's field. For the girl who keeps rabbits up the street. The kids all keep watch to see if the mean old lady will see us. Every kid is living in fear and ready to run. What are you doing there! – you kids get out of that field! I run in terror along with the other fugitives.

To be a young man

A boy who fears falling off a bridge.
A poet whose heart could not be burned.
A dump-truck leaning over towards a house.

who is blinded

Do you assume that everybody dreams?
Are you – would you say – a person who dreams a lot?
Are you a person who is aware of the nature of your dreams?

by the sun.

A group of kids shovelling snow on a pond.
Three kids on their way to Sunday School.
A young man making architectural drawings.

Walking over to the pond. Skates draped on laces around our necks. Carry-

ing our hockey sticks. Some extra pucks in our pockets in case one gets lost –
you can't have a game without a puck. It's going to be a perfect day. The air is
clear and cold. Blue sky and fluffy white clouds. No snow on the ground since
the last thaw. A perfect day for a game of hockey on Pinafore Pond.

A cold coming we had of it.

There's something clear and clean about Camus. *L'Étranger* is the most
intriguing book I have read. Meursault never explains himself nor does Camus. It just says that this is life and these are the questions. It's the nearest
book I have read to *Oedipus the King.*

He didn't play Minor Hockey in his final year. University took up his time.
Then his brother said why not play in the Industrial League. A bunch of guys
who shoot the puck around once a week. It was a way to get some needed
exercise.

"Walter Davies was a Barnardo Boy whose father gave him up for a better
life."

"Walter was only twelve years old when he and his brother were sent to
Canada."

And how am I, then, guilty? I did not come here from nowhere. I did not
marry the widowed Queen. I did not solve a riddle which only a seer could
solve. I have merely been an onlooker. Held my tongue as I sat at the feasts. I
have never been one to hold an opinion at all. Kings are bubbles blown by the
gods. What makes him think that I would want to be king?

*Some of the stories - mix them in a jar - was part of a boat - lots of things
to think about - nice to look back - hadn't thought about it - what we are - get
it free again - what it means to all of us - introduce a whole new topic.*

Old Doc is a cork on the surface of life.
Old Doc is a self-made zygote.
Old Doc is the man who invented the revolving door.

*How many words
can be found
in a barrel of ink?*

"The rider-less horse is a time-honoured symbol of the soldier who has
fallen in the midst of the action. The President's widow stands with her children as the catafalque passes by. Young John-John gives his father a salute."

Settling back into our routine. Fivey on the sidewalk handing up cans, me
in the back building a load and Herm inching along behind the wheel. Not too

heavy on the streets we passed as we went to the dump and back. Didn't see any other trucks at the dump. Ivan was down the other end with the bulldozer so we couldn't ask him what the other guys were saying. We'll just take her as she comes. If it doesn't get heavier as we go on, we should be okay.

There's a divinity that shapes our ends.

I am early on the job. A couple of weeks into my first year. Frank and I are collecting on Sunset Drive. The Cold Storage place. Frank is in the truck. A woman comes out to talk to me as I'm emptying her cans. Last week, someone put a dent in one of my cans. I was on the streets last week, so I say it wasn't me. She says someone dented her can. She says that maybe she should call the office and I say that would be a good idea. That's the best way to find out who was on this route. The boss comes over to me at noon-hour. Were you at the Cold Storage this morning, John? A lady called and said she tried to talk to a young fellow but he kept sassing her back. Just what exactly did you say that made her so mad?

So perhaps he would just be a voice, like Dylan Thomas. Chanting imagery in the tones of an ancient bard. The enchanting Christmas times of early childhood. Heart-felt words to an old man at the end of his life. If he had lived differently, he would still be alive today.

Starting to build our second load of the morning.

Margaret Street - Hughes Street - Elizabeth Street - Coyne Street - Balaclava Street.

No doubt I am what everyone in Verona considers to be an admirable catch. The interview with her family will be a mere formality – a matter of words. As for Juliet – she is exquisite – she will be a worthy wife for me. In my household she will be the very crown. Her presentation at the Capulet ball made for an evening I shall never forget. I was so enamored I almost climbed the orchard wall. But time will soon be favourable – I have only to bide my time. No expense will be spared for the nuptials – our two lives will begin on that day. Juliet will make the sweetest blushing bride.

Visiting all of the factories - put it in the bank - a perfect day for a game - no questions asked - as if they are real - just point out the facts - the day is getting dark - look into your heart - until the sun comes out again - ahead all is dark.

What does the mirror say about Old Doc?
Has he ever peered inside?
What does the mirror say on the other side of the wall?

He was the first

to tell a story
around a campfire.

We sit down where the rink used to be. Just a faint outline, now, of melted snow. The last thaw covered the pond with a sheet of water. Now it's frozen into the best ice we ever saw. None of the other kids are here so far. We take off our boots and lace up our skates. Hey, what do you say we chase the puck. We'll be able to skate for miles. We can go way back to the creek that feeds the pond.

The sedge has withered from the lake.

Stopping for ice-cream on the way back home from Port Stanley. Mom and Dad let us pick whatever we want. They let you come into the store in your bathing suit, but we always change at the cottage. I always pick black-cherry every time. Oh – and a napkin so it doesn't drip on the seat of the car.

A lady who rolls her eyes towards the sky.
A person who knows every street in town.
A hockey player in search of the Stanley Cup.

Why does every reader feel that he is Hamlet? Why does a viewer see himself when he watches that play? What did Shakespeare know that very few writers seem to know?

Gradually, my eyes adjust.
I am seeing the lady now.
She is nervous and looking straight ahead.
At the bright light in the ring.

Ever dream that you are on a treadmill?
Ever dream that you are a person who is trapped in a box?
Ever dream of yourself – adrift – in a boat in the raging current above Niagara Falls?

"The ceremony on Parliament Hill, in Ottawa, was a culmination of a year and more of special events which were designed to celebrate this country and what it means to all of us. It is almost a year ago since the Prime Minister lit the Centennial Flame that burns, so brightly, today. From Expo 67, to the Centennial Train, to the Voyageur Canoe Pageant, to the totem-carvings in British Columbia, to the fishing derbies in Newfoundland, there has been a constant pageant of events – like signal-bonfires – all across this land. Every province, city and town has been hosting special events from coast to coast to coast. People from many nations have chosen 1967 as the year to visit Canada. There was even, in New York City, a Canada Day."

There must be birds
who have no voice-box,
though for the life of me
I can't think of one.

He grew up and went to high school.

I wander around Banff. A beautiful little town. Nestled in the mountains. A tourist town, but completely unspoiled. Hey – what am I thinking? – I'm a tourist too.

A newspaper clipping with a story about a boxer.
A mayor and council in session.
A class of students doing a science experiment.

Grandpa Davies and the Christmas cake. Sent from Scotland by a fellow Royal Marine. Soak it with brandy and strike a match. Turn out the lights in the dining room. All the Passfield and Davies faces glow in the dark.

"It was a warm and sunny day. President Kennedy addressed the nation and the world, and spoke words of boldness, of vision, and of resolve. 'To achieve the goal, before this decade is out, of landing a man on the Moon.' "

So – building a load again. The same routine – the same results. Build the clean bags into a wall across the dump-box. Save your boxes and fill them with things that have some weight. When you get enough, you wedge the boxes across the back. Dump the cans over the wall into the front of the open dump-box. Then make a wall along the side right to the back. Then keep your feet out of the wet stuff as you block off and fill the hole that you left at the door. When she's full, you take her down and dump her again.
A shape with a lion body and the head of a man.
Getting done early, one day, on the streets. Dumping the final load and going to work in the truck-garage. Taking a wheel with a flat tire and a sledge hammer and a long-handled spoon and prying the tire off the rim by whacking the rubber with the sledge to break it loose. Then putting some air in the tube and putting the tube in the tub of water to find the hole. Marking the hole with chalk and then scraping the tube with a cheese-type grater and putting a patch on the hole by using the electrical device that melts the patch and makes a seal. Then putting the tube in the tire and the tire back on the rim and then wrapping the wheel with two chains and filling her with air. The two chains are in case the tire blows up in my face.

And of course there were people he would get to work with year-round. There was Herm – who lived alone in a tiny room in the Park House and seemed to spend his evenings nursing a beer. And there was Bumps – who'd spent too many years as an amateur boxer and had to hang on to the sides of the truck like a fisherman in a storm as it crept along the curb, because he couldn't keep his balance anymore. And there was Fivey – who'd lost his arm in a terrible accident, and always called out to anyone he knew in town – and he knew everyone – "Hey Stumpy! – or Hey Lumpy! – or Hey Dumpy! – Wouldn't a tall cool one go good right about now?"

I always assumed that a story just told a story – a series of events that happened to the people in the book.

I have always trusted my father. I have trusted my brother as well. But now – I wonder whether there is anyone whom I can trust at all. I no longer understand Hamlet. Was he ever the boy that I once thought him to be? What do these letters mean to me now? – what do these letters mean to him? The ink is still wet on the pages – still warm. I tie them up with a ribbon. What will he say when I offer them back to him?

Never writes anything down - might be a problem - someone in the dark - walking down the path - clutch the steering-wheel - not everything was spoken - like an aztec artisan - gettin' her done on time - the process of reading - a better set of wheels.

Old Doc collected hair-tonic. Used to find the bottles in the garbage. The first time he yanked the truck door open and held up a green-glass bottle and said 'Hair tonic!' and shoved it behind the seat, I assumed that he wanted it for his hair.

I got to thinking that I'd never seen Old Doc without a hat. Might look pretty sharp with a shave and a nice suit. I tried to picture Doc with his imaginary hair all slicked back and nicely combed.

Wasn't too long – a few more houses – and Old Doc yanked the truck door open. He pulled the bottle of hair tonic out from behind the seat and unscrewed the top and took a swig. Then I knew that he wasn't thinking about his hair.

If you lie
on the earth
at midnight.

Chasing the puck for miles and miles. Just my brother and me and that's all. Nobody else has arrived for the Saturday hockey game. Once in a while the ice makes a noise. A hollow boom or a creaking sound. That just means that it's expanding as the air gets cold. We pass the puck back and forth. If we miss it, we skate to catch up. It bounces over the little pebbles on the surface of the pond. The perfect ice on the perfect winter day.

And drunk the milk of paradise.

Ibsen and the interaction of the past and the present. *A Doll's House – Hedda Gabler – The Wild Duck* and all the rest. But I don't care for the basic premise. It makes for an interesting interaction of the past and the present. But I don't see life as the present being poisoned by the past.

He could spend a summer in a rustic cottage. Go for strolls on the Yorkshire moors. Soak himself in the wind and rain of the Brontës. Get an idea for a plot and some characters. Write a novel that would resemble *Wuthering Heights.*

Getting into the rhythm of our second load.
1st Avenue - Antrim Street - Cedar Street - Elysian Street - John Street.

Grandpa Davies only spoke once about his adventures. He would sit in the rocking chair on the porch of Uncle Claude's house and say nothing at all. Just a question or two about how I was doing in school. "When he starts to thump his hand on the arm of the rocker, it's time to leave," my mom would always say. But that time when our grandpa was sick, and couldn't climb the stairs, and stayed at our house for a week, he told of getting stuck in the ice in the harbour at Archangel after the war, and having to carry all his kit on his back on the frozen trails. He never spoke – even once – about Gallipoli. It was Mom who told us he was there. I would have liked to hear him talk about it, but you never asked an old soldier about the war.

Wants something more - no axe to grind - waiting for her turn - from a particular day - the other things that count - hightail it out of there - intense negotiations - mingled and chatted - my personal feast - hidden under the cardboard.

Old Doc was gone for a week. When he came back, he purred like a tomcat.

"The boss was lookin' for me but he never figured out where I was. He was askin' all over town but nobody knew. And I wasn't tellin' nobody neither. I got me a neat little hidin' place. I was shacked up with a nice little lady. She didn't tell nobody neither. I took my last pay and bought some supplies and we hunkered down. If you wanted, you could call it a honeymoon.

"I sez to the boss – the day I come back – 'You didn't have no clue where I was, did you now?' 'No,' the boss sez, 'I didn't, Doc – I had no idea in hell where you were. Now get to work an' make up for all that lost time.' "

*The man's beloved
had sailed the sea
in a ship*

*which was slowly
approaching the shore.*

"Behind me, the soldiers are setting fire to the huts of some of the Vietnamese peasants. They are thought to be Vietnamese who are sympathetic to the Northern side. A soldier reported the possibility that gunfire might have originated from the direction of these huts."

What would the boss say if I wrote about the garbage? Should I ask for his permission before I write? I wouldn't mind if he said 'no', but I wouldn't want him telling me what or what not to write.

Stains the white radiance of eternity.

On special pickup at the stores. Backing up to the upholstery store. Frank goes in to talk to the owner and I open up the lid on the bin they have outside. Suddenly! – what was that! – was that a rat? It was gone before I knew it! – it leaped out of the bin and almost grazed my arm! What if it had gone for my throat? Do rats attack humans? The old upholstery is all packed in here in a pile. All the stuffings of all the old sofas and chairs. You have to pull it out in hand-fulls and dump it into the bucket on the back of the truck. I take the shovel off the rack on the truck and bang on the upholstery bin and stand back but I don't see any more rats. Now to dig my hands in the upholstery and drag it out. Would it be best if I work with eyes open or keep them shut?

"The two Davies boys worked on a farm near St. Thomas."
"When Walter was eighteen years old he went back to England again."

Two chemicals

*Blanks on a map that one yearns to see.
The CBC evening news.
Barrels of oil sloshing in a truck.*

mixing

Ever find yourself dreaming as you go about your daily chores?
Would you consider that you have both dreams and nightmares?
Are nightmares reserved for the night and dreams for the day?

in a jar.

Turning around and heading back. We went up Turtle Alley and then we headed up to where the creek becomes the pond. Houses and farms up on the hills, but we don't see anyone. No snow so we can always find the puck. The game might be a problem because there's no snow on the sides to contain the puck. If you shoot it hard it will skitter away for miles. But we can take turns chasing the puck and bringing it back. We'll use our boots to make the goals. Other kids will be coming as well. When someone comes, they'll join a side. When someone leaves, we'll even up. Soon the whole rink will be swarming with skates and sticks. We'll play hockey until it's too dark to see the puck.

Was this the face that launched a thousand ships?

The end of Grade Eight seemed to come very soon. A parent shouted 'bean-pole' over the boards at a hockey game, and I knew he meant me. A tall gawky kid in the back row in the final assembly. We don't have a gym, so the parents and the graduating kids all cram into the front foyer. My dad helped me tie my tie on my Sunday suit. The music teacher asked me and Robbie not to sing. It's a beautiful, beautiful song. It always brings the tears to my eyes. Just perfect for this occasion. So you two just move your lips as if you are singing the words, but make sure that no sound comes out. That way you won't spoil it for the parents.

Chapter 7

Old cans of paint and other junk. If there was more we could leave the whole lot for special pickup. Then the homeowner would have to pay extra and by the look of the house, they don't have a lot of money to spare. Must have bought the house and cleaned the basement out. Anyway – I can use these cans to weigh down the loose paper and light boxes, so we'll take it with no questions asked – their lucky day.

And saw the skull beneath the skin.

Learned a lot in high school. But I was painfully, painfully shy. I never spoke out in class – pretended I didn't know the answers so I wouldn't have to talk. The kids all thought I was stupid, but the teachers could see my work. Didn't join one club or play one extra-curricular sport. Just played hockey at the arena and on the pond. Discovered books – a cache – a mother-lode – in the high school library. *Boy on Defense,* by Scott Young. Lloyd Percival and all the secrets of the hockey trade. Went with my parents to the public library once a week. Liked the English classes, but didn't like anything else. Math and Science seemed to have me by the throat.

To be a young man

Pavilions from every country in the world.
A man receiving therapy on his arm.
A boy throwing hay-bales onto a truck.

who has graduated

So what good are dreams and nightmares to you?
What is their primary function in your thoughts?
Do they serve to buoy you up or to drag you down?

 from university.

A young man reading a book on the beach.

A family roasting hotdogs over a fire.
A black car moving like a beetle.

How can people live through a war? My parents and grandparents lived through two. And the Great Depression as well. All the History is in the books. We seem to live – now – outside of time. John F. Kennedy was History for us – a rocket bursting into flame. We turned away from History – as from a grenade.

Who are these coming to the sacrifice?

Death of a Salesman should be interesting. Don't know whether I would have put it on the course. In some ways, it's just another teenage-rebellion story. Reject the old fogies and take over your life for yourself. Very, very American, I would say. Always fighting the Revolution over again. But – hate your dad; love your dad. There's actually a maturity that's built right in. If we can get beneath the surface, it could work quite well.

Well, a scout was in the arena. From one of the teams in the NHL. He was looking for exceptional talent. Came right into the dressing room. "Looks like you could step on the ice in the major leagues."

"There is a massive monument in the churchyard of the Old St. Thomas Church."

"It commemorates the seven members of a pioneer family who died of cholera within seven years."

I am a wizard in my laboratory! I know the magic formula! It came to me – blindingly – in a flash! I now know Ingredient A and Ingredient B! All I have to do is to mix them in a jar!

Didn't always come alive - how many layers - eyes were ripe for pain - felt that he was himself - don't invite paupers - waiting in the aisle - unless I get more building materials - enter another world - I'm a tourist too - lose a lot of time.

And Ray.
What about Ray?
Do the days string together for Ray or is each day a thing apart?

"None,"
said the
pessimist.

Every day the Russian bombers fly northward. Every day the Russian bombers turn and go back. Every day the American bombers fly northward. Every day the American bombers turn and go back. If they meet it will be in the sky above Canada. Both sides turn before they reach the North Pole.

So foul and fair a day I have not seen.

My job as a newspaper boy, during the winter. There are people who don't always pay. Their tickets remain in my account-book for week after week. How much do I owe you?– really? – that much? – can you come back on Wednesday? Don't have any change right now – can I catch you next week? The only problem is that I have to pay at the office. I can't refuse to deliver the paper and the office charges me for every one. And there's a man who always tells me that I am late. I tell him the truck doesn't come in the morning until six o'clock. I tell him I'll bring him a paper just as soon as I open the bundle. Then, I'll go back to the restaurant and start to deliver the rest.

If only I had the voice of a Richard Burton. I listen to his Hamlet-record almost every day. He used to practice speaking as Hamlet with a heavy weight on his chest. He left the stage to act in films and marry a movie star. Wonder what he sounds like when he orders a drink on a plane?

Wondering how the second load is going to go.

Barnes Street - Forest Avenue - Parkside Drive - Spruce Street - Tecumseh Street.

I am a wizard in my laboratory! I have Ingredient A and Ingredient B! But now, I need to find another secret formula! I have been working through the nights and through the days! Now I need to invent a magic mixing-bowl!

Surrounded by flame - the jar was always full - earliest childhood memory - have me by the throat - the life that people see - fish on the surface - so easily be displaced - just a lucky guess - a matter of words - fill up a page or two.

Ray has a wife and kids.

Ray's wife comes in early on paydays and drops Ray off and the brakes squeal as the kids lean out the windows of the car.

And she comes back early at noon to get Ray's pay-cheque so she can take it up to the bank to cash so she can buy the groceries for the family meals.

He told a fib
that would last
for thousands of years.

Garbage men never talk. Of course you have a job to do. You don't work all that close. And during the lunch break it's always a crowd – ten or twelve or sometimes fifteen – so all they talk about is how heavy or light the garbage is today. Do they talk to their wives and kids when they get home? What does Herm say, in the Park House, late at night?

No! I am not Prince Hamlet, nor was meant to be.

Biff is about thirty-five. Once, he was a teenager. He had the world by the seat of the pants. He was a high school football hero. All the girls hung around the house. His friends would always sweep out the furnace room. His younger brother looked up to him. His mother did the washing and made the meals. But then something went wrong. Biff failed Math and went to talk about it with his dad.

A lady who dies of breast cancer.
A maid who is wiser than her master.
A person collecting driftwood on the shore.

Why does the story of Gatsby and Daisy have such resonance? While other stories of gangsters simply do not? Did Fitzgerald know what he was writing or was it just a lucky guess? – a leap in the dark?

She is wearing heavy makeup.
She has sparkles in her hair.
She is wearing an outfit with spangles.
Little glimpses flash in the dark.

Are there layers of thought in the mind?
How many layers would you guess that there are?
How many would you say are accessible to you?

"The Passfield family spent the day on the beach at Port Stanley. Port Stanley is on Lake Erie, about twenty miles across the lake from the USA. The water was warm and the sun shone all day. They swam and lay on towels and relaxed and talked all morning and all afternoon. All day there were people strolling along the beach."

Is it not the giraffe
who has no voice
to laugh or to sing?

He wasn't very good at Math and Science.

Spending a wonderful day in Banff. Right in the heart of the Rocky Mountains. The Cave and Basin, the Hot Springs, Sulphur Mountain, the Banff Springs Hotel. Banff Indian Days – I sit on the bleachers right up at the fence. Plenty to see and do in the town of Banff.

A boy delivering newspapers in the dark.
A bent basketball-stand in a schoolyard.

A father telling stories of his days out West.

Three little boys with sore stomachs. Stole an onion from a store uptown. Made a plan to steal an apple. Tommy grabbed a cooking-onion instead. We climb to the roof of Bobby's garage and pass the onion around. The tears stream down our cheeks and our stomachs churn.

Paint your main character into a corner – then figure out a way to get him out again. Writing is as easy as painting the floor of a house. In a tragedy, there will be footprints in the paint. In a comedy, the paint will be – miraculously – dry.

You know only a heap of broken images.

My one-day job selling tickets for service stations. Knocking on doors up and down the streets in Chatham. The gas station is under new management and people don't know the owner at all. Nobody wants to buy a block of tickets from a boy they don't know. The older boy in the car drives up and down slowly, while the rest of us knock on doors. Ten dollars for a ticket – a number of car washes, a number of cleanings, a number of changes of oil. Cheaper if you buy a ticket than if you pay for each service on its own. I stand at the door and explain that this is a wonderful deal.

Herm always told the same two jokes. Whenever he saw a dog, he would say: "Hey Bud" – Herm addressed everyone as 'Bud' – "that there's a black-smith dog – give him a kick in the ass and he'll make a bolt for the door!"; and whenever Herm saw an old mattress – or an old rusty bedspring – or a bedstead that someone didn't want any more, Herm would say, as he handed it up to the back of the truck – "Hey Bud – Take up thy bed and walk."

And all of the stories that I read in elementary school and high school and university were about people who lived somewhere else.

I am a wizard in my laboratory! I need a formula for a jar! I have tried glass and stone and crockery! Time after time I pour Ingredient A into Ingredient B! But the container just dissolves and melts away!

Garbage smell so sweet - not take no days off - a grim look on her face - the whole house of cards - what sort of future - the excitement of the occasion - your work will be vital - asks the same question - cannot understand why - people whose lives we can live.

When is Ray going to buy those brake-shoes?
What does Ray think of his wife and kids?
Does Ray string all the days together or keep them apart?

On the grass
behind your house.

Boys playing marbles and little girls skipping. A little old lady with her groceries in a cart. Churchill Crescent – Dieppe Drive. Balaclava Street and Trafalgar Street. Some of these streets you can date by reading a history book. Why didn't somebody in St. Thomas write a book like *War and Peace*?
And put his life between the judge's lips.
Willie is a man of about sixty – or sixty-five. He sees himself as a hot-shot salesman. But he ends up losing his job. The son of his old boss tells him to hand in his sample-case and not come to work anymore. Willie has a son named Happy. He has a wife and a house. He has a son named Biff who has come back home. Biff is going to go into town to ask for a job. Willie plans to meet his two sons for lunch downtown.

Maybe there might be another Great Depression. Leave St. Thomas and ride the rails. Find out what it's like to be down and desperate. Keep a diary of all that he saw. Write a novel along the lines of *The Grapes of Wrath*.

The second load is building very fast.
Wellington Street - Trafalgar Street - Edgeware Road - Manitoba Street - Gliddon Avenue.

"John's marks are not as high as they could be. He has attributes that he is not using to the full. He seems to have a reluctance to apply himself to such subjects as Mathematics and Science, but he does quite well in Spelling and Composition. Although shy, he gets along well with the others in the class. Testing shows that he would be good at clerical work."

No limousine arrives - exchanged thoughts - he couldn't jump and run - do all birds sing - a really excellent day - depths which we seldom see - would stir his blood - is it hallowe'en - teaching me to sharpen - someone will dig them up.

Ray had a beat-up old car. Another married man with a wife and kids. His brakes would squeal so loud that you had to cover your ears – the brake-pads had been worn right down to the metal.
"Can't afford to buy new ones this week. Couple more pay-cheques and I'll put on new ones myself. Had a few close calls on the way to work – have a few tonight on my way home.
"I already borrowed from the boss so I can't do that. An' there ain't no bus that goes all the way out to where I live. Just have to take her easy, that's all it means. Drive defensively, and hope the other guy stops.
"When the transmission quit, I had to hitchhike, but I ain't doin' that no

more. Alls I need is a new set of brakes. It's pay-cheque to pay-cheque even when you got a job."

"The ship
is the least important element
in the voyage,"
thought the man on shore –
and the ship began to sink.

I should just write the article and put it in a drawer. *How To Build a Perfect Load of Garbage.* A little art and a little science. Like an Aztec artisan working on a wall. The skills and knowledge that one acquires as one learns the job.
After life's fitful fever he sleeps well.
My summer in the Militia. The St. Thomas Armouries. We sit in a briefing room. The Sergeant-major is giving a talk. Your work will be vital after the drop takes place. The enemy will target the largest population zones. The atomic-bomb will wipe out all of the major facilities. Everyone here – in this room – will be assigned to traffic control. You will be stationed on the periphery of target-zero. You will inform the fleeing populous as to where to access the necessities – such as shelter and food. The roads will be busy after the bomb is dropped, so you will be busy as well. Many thousands will flee the contamination zone.

"The only survivor of the pioneer family left St. Thomas and struck it rich when he invested in a silver mine."
"He came back and built the monument in the old St. Thomas churchyard – to commemorate his family for all of time."

A nut

An English family tasting peanut butter.
Digging something up after thousands of years.
Poets who failed at writing poetic plays.

buried by a squirrel

Are there layers of the mind that are inaccessible?
Great depths of murky water down below?
Do you dream of a cork lazily drifting on the tide?

underground.

How old would Herman be, I wonder. Jeez – if he started in Toronto, on the garbage wagon – pulled by horses – at age eighteen – how old would he be? Did someone say it was during the First World War? – or am I just imagin-ing that? We had horses pulling the bread-wagon and the milk-wagon on our street when everybody who lived on the street had a car. So maybe it wasn't all that long ago. If it was forty years ago, he'd be fifty-eight years old. If it was fifty years ago, he'd be sixty-eight and able to retire. With the way he lives his life, it's hard to tell. Was there a calendar in his room? – I wonder if he's checking off the days.

Pray tell me, sir, whose dog are you?

This is a painful book to read. Biff can't stand Willie. Willie can't stand Biff. They always fight whenever they are together. They yearn for each other whenever they are apart. What happened when they were younger? Why do relationships fall apart? All of this makes me think about my father. Thank you, Sir, for putting this book on the course.

Chapter 8

Turning the corner and starting on a new street. Always rows and rows of cans. Houses on both sides of the street. Maple trees with the branches stretching out over the parked cars. Cars hiding the cans, but we find them anyway. And if you let your eyes go far enough, there's cans on both sides stretching all the way to the end of your sight. Forgot to turn back and look as we left the last street. Always nice to look back and see miles of empty cans.

A bracelet of bright hair about the bone.

I am in the doctor's office. He puts the stethoscope on my chest and asks me to cough. So what do you expect to be when you grow up, he asks me. I don't know what to say so I say, I like words. You like words? Yes. Well, that's interesting, he says, and taps my chest.

To be a citizen

A workman building a wall of garbage.
A book about the rituals of a culture,
A wily old veteran still playing the game.

who seeks to change

So what is the process of reading a book?
What the reward for turning the page?
Do you enter another world or enter your own?

the social system.

Oil barrels leaking from a truck.
A woman cashing a cheque at a bank.
A squad of soldiers marching on a parade square.

Up on Talbot Street – at the remains of the John Scott Tavern. A raging fire here, about a month ago. The big blackened timbers all fell down into the cellar-hole. The boss's son will operate the work-bull – the big rubber-tired bulldozer with the massive bucket on the front. The job is to clear the lot and haul everything down to the dump. The first thing is to separate the framing-timbers from the smaller timbers that supported the floor-boards. This old tavern must have been here for a least a hundred and fifty years.

Until death tramples it to fragments.

There's the Odeon, the Capital and the Columbia. Fifteen cents for the first two – for the Columbia only a dime. We take the bus uptown and buy a box of popcorn. *The Bowery Boys – Tarzan – Ma and Pa Kettle on the Farm.* Kids throw popcorn boxes up into the air. Stand at attention for the Queen. Pretend we're riding horses all the way home.

He was in awe at the try-out camp. All these hockey stars on the ice. Cyclone Taylor, Howie Morenz, Teeder Kennedy, Rocket Richard. How would he be able to skate with these guys? These were giants in the world of professional sports.

"Mary Park Passfield was a widow in St. Thomas with five young children."

"She cleaned houses and catered to the wealthy to make ends meet."

I go every day to the trial. Meursault looks at me but I never know what he is thinking. He told me once that he loved me, but I have never been sure that he knows what that means. I could never be a witness. I don't know why he shot the gun. It's a part of his life of which I know nothing at all. Oh why do I go there every day? It is a question that I am always asking of myself. Who can explain the feelings that seize control of our hearts?

The things that i have come to know - run over by a truck - you should try that - separate the framing timbers - disappear and never return - i wrench the wheel - something i want to say - in case the tire blows up - what is it that they know - how well do you know.

Oh – the family again! – why do you want to hear about that? – because the manuals say you should write about what you know? Oh I have plenty of pleasant memories – I'm not a particularly morbid guy – I could write a *Sunshine Sketches*, I suppose. The little town in the sunshine, called St. Thomas – here the people are like people all over the world – whatever happens anywhere can happen here.

My dad sat with we kids at the kitchen table. He read his diary from the West – when he was only twenty-three – and went out to be a cowboy and work on the farms. And he told these wonderful stories and we kids were just enthralled – to think our dad had done these things so long ago.

And our mom would talk of England, when she was just a little girl. And of the Guildhall in the ancient market town. And how the Davies kids would go for walks with their Grandad – Henry Kennett – and stop in a village and he would buy them a lemonade.

"All,"
said the
optimist.

"It is a dull day here in Washington, as we witness this sombre November event. One can't help thinking as the catafalque passes by. Of the ebullience, the optimism, the sense of life having a positive purpose, as the President took office such a short time ago."

Going figure-skating with my sister and her friends. A group of girls in the back of a car. A parent comes and gets us at our school at four o'clock. Making figures in the ice. A perfect circle – a perfect figure-eight. I'll never be as good as the others are.
All breathing human passion far above.
That job painting the rooms of a house. Dennis and I resume our painting. The man comes to the bottom of the stairs and shouts – Dennis! – really angry and really loud. Dennis looks at me and shrugs and climbs down the ladder and puts his paint brush down and goes down the stairs. I continue painting the windows. Maybe Dennis will want to switch when we work in the other rooms – me on the ladder painting the curlicues and Dennis on the windows – and then later we can both work on the walls. Dennis comes back upstairs and stands there for a moment and then he says, He's really, really mad! – he wants you fired!

Or Orson Welles when he appears on television. The perfect timbre to in-tone the voice of God. He could make the phone book sound like the voice of doom. *The War of the Worlds* is in my record-collection. Some day I hope I'll get to see *Citizen Kane*.

Some streets are heavy – some are light.
Yarmouth Road - Weldon Avenue - St. George Street - Moore Street - Erie Street.

For the life of me, I cannot understand why Nora persists in acting with such immaturity. She insists that she can live on her own. She has lost the ability to see herself as a child. Her father guided her in their home – I have guided her in ours. And now she has the idea that she can guide herself. I have made a few insignificant errors. But Nora has made a series of terrible blunders. She almost caused our happy home to come crashing down. How can a woman possibly live without a man?

Unsure as to how to go about it - if you sailed too far - what is the point - a movement at my elbow - get beneath the surface - leap right up off the page - reached up to the sky - I should walk away - take her as she comes - accessible to you.

And my brother working for the summers. Drawing architectural plans. The boss trusted him when he showed what he could do.

And my sister and her shiny new sports car. A brand new Triumph Spitfire – painted a beautiful racing-blue. And she bought it with her own money from her very first job.

And our Grandpa telling stories – just the once – to my brother and I. He was sick and staying at our house for a week or two. About his days in the Royal Navy – how they had to abandon their ship which was trapped in the ice.

He yielded
to the urge
to tell a tall-tale.

So I'll run the work-bull, says the boss's son, while you attach the chain to the timbers from the floor. Hook her on the bucket and then jump down there and wrap the chain around a timber and then jump aside. And then I'll yank the work-bull back and raise the bucket and the chain'll rip the floor-timbers off the frame. Then jump back in again and do the same. We'll just work our way along 'til we get her done. Like stripping the bones off an ancient dinosaur.

Nor set down aught in malice.

Conrad and the past and the present. *Heart of Darkness* and *Lord Jim*. Inter-layering what happened then with what's happening now. Parallels and contrasts as the thoughts that these experiences suggest.

A person rolling down a car's windows.
A person conducting an imaginary interview.
A person ordering macaroni in a restaurant.

"Load every rift of your subject with ore." What subject? – what rift? – what ore? Is there a way to figure out what all of this means?

She is wearing heavy makeup.
She must be beautiful underneath.
She is plastered in white powder.
I can barely see her face.

What have these authors dredged up from the depths?
What have they managed to put on the page?

What do all these gallons of ink have to say?

"The Mayor of St. Thomas and the Council were in attendance for the celebration at City Hall. Every public building – and many of the stores and houses – were decorated with flags. There was a parade on Talbot Street with many patriotic floats and marching bands. There were concerts in all the parks around the town. All of St. Thomas was in attendance. The *St. Thomas Times-Journal* put out a Centennial issue of the newspaper with pictures and captions of all the events around town."

What does the platypus
have to say? –
Does he ever
make a noise?

He told the family doctor that he was interested in words.

I take the bus back to Lake Louise Station. I get there at eight o'clock. Only one other person on the bus, but he stays on. Only a tiny, dim light on the platform. The door to Lake Louise Station is tightly locked!

A group of kids pretending to be cowboys.
Two boys digging a grave beside a church.
A cold-storage locker for winter clothes.

Uncle Claude and the salt-and-pepper shakers. Ranged around the shelf high up on the cottage wall. At first, he collected them on his travels – each set reminded him of a place he had been. Then people started to bring them as gifts, and the concept was lost. Some he has to put away when the minister comes.

"Within the past two years – 1966 and 1967 – we have had a number of amazing photographs from space. We have had the first image of Earth from the Moon's orbit, the first image of Earth from the Moon's surface, and the first full-disk colour pictures of the Earth. We have seen ourselves from a perspective from which humankind has never been able to see itself before."

If it rains while you're collecting garbage, you just have to work right through. You've got the hours and you've got the garbage, and it has to come off. Oh, you can sit in the cab for ten minutes or so, during the heaviest part of the downpour, but if it doesn't let up, there's nothing you can do. You have to get back out on the street and collect the garbage. You'd roast if you wore a raincoat, so you don't wear one of those. You'll be cold and wet until the sun comes out again.

Then reached the caverns measureless to man.

That time when I didn't get the job. Sitting in an outer-office in a factory in London. Listening to two people in the inner-office chatting about their vacations plans. Well we always go up to the cottage – but that can get boring after a while. So maybe we'll throw a few clothes in the car and hit the road. Take in the sights in some of the cities. Lots of Centennial projects this year. Feeling stifled in the office – getting tired of the heavy load. Get away from this factory for a while and breathe some fresh air.

But on the other hand – it hadn't always been so easy being a garbage man. There was that time he'd been told to take the little truck to the welder's. So he'd gone into the truck-garage and backed her out and turned the steering-wheel a little too sharply and there was a loud crack! crack! crack! crack! crack! as the front bumper tore the moulding off the door-frame of the truck-garage. And all the men were on lunch hour, just about to go back to work, and they all looked at him as he climbed out of the truck and stood there. And he looked at the shattered garage-door moulding as the boss said, "No John – I meant the *little* truck – the one over there."

So I was learning, when I read these stories, about what it would have been like to live in other places and at other times.

I try to ignore the scratching at the window. I concentrate on these words. Can one discern a distinct personality in a scrawl? Well, here the writing is as fine as one could imagine. Minute – precise – measured. But the words – oh my, the words. There was a heart of fire which beat in this anxious breast. I must be careful or I will burn my fingers. Can one be warmed by the blood of years ago?

A noble profession - the green light shining - visited upon one - was there a calendar - a piece of clean white paper - it is a question - there is much confusion - collecting drift-wood - the discarded packing-crates - deeper inside our own minds.

Oh I have dozens of pleasant memories. Just diving into the waves in the lake at Port Stanley would fill up a page or two. And the Sunday School picnics, at Pinafore Park, with the games and the food.

My wife-to-be and I travelled to Expo 67 – just this spring – as chaperones. We took a bus with the kids of her school to Montreal. The whole thing was spectacular – our feet were very sore – we visited every pavilion from every country in the world.

Or how we met at a summer youth camp. We hit it off from the very start – we found we have the same sense of humour and all the other things that count. My sister invited me along – I took a week off at the end of last summer, before

I went back to school – and that's where the two of us met.

The sap
will enter into
your veins.

Blackened timbers and shards of glass. Broken crockery and splintered boards. The debris from one hundred and fifty years of serving beer. I have work-boots on, but try to keep an eye for rusty old spikes and nails. I wrap the chain around a beam and I move away. He jerks the work-bull back and a floor-timber shudders and lets go. Then I jump back in the debris and wrap the chain around and he jerks the chain again. Every time I wrap the chain, he yanks at another timber. I'm working up a sweat – there's rusty nails all through the debris and my feet might slip. The faster I work, the faster he yanks, and the faster I jump in and jump out again. This goes on for timber after timber – the work-bull rips at board after board. He's going to kill me, I think to myself. What if the chain lets go and wraps around my neck? More sweat, more speed, more plunging into and out of the blackened debris! I should walk away before I get carried out on a board!

Wragg is in custody.

I stand up and leave the room. The teacher asked me to stay after the bell. I'm not going to stay and I'm not going to tell him who it was. I did not put the tack on the girl's seat.

He would take a trip to Athens. Sit in the theatre and close his eyes. The sun would stir his blood as it fired the souls of the Ancient Greeks. A story of fate and pride and revenge. He would write a play in the manner of Sophocles.

Hard to tell if we are going to finish by noon.
Hepburn Avenue - Flora Street - Edgeware Line - Cypress Street - Centre Street.

Uncle Claude has a good life now, but he had his problems in the early days. He started work in a brick yard shortly after the Davies family came to Canada. Then he got a job in an iron foundry – hard and dirty work and not very well paid. He had finished school in England and was scrubbing pots and pans. Then his family came out here and he worked on a farm. He belonged to one of those book clubs, when he was young, for a number of years. They would send a book a month for him to read. *War and Peace* and all the classics on the shelves at the cottage. What he had then and what he has now – travelling everywhere in the world and making friends. Wonder if Uncle Claude ever thinks of writing things down.

Going to have to walk - a whole new way of life - what do i know - walk around all day - all should have done the same - riding for a fall - over the brim - keep himself high and dry - images on a string - coming up big.

Oh I could go on and on and on. We have two families – the Davies and the Passfields – so there's always lots going on. And there's five in our own family – so there's plenty of stories to tell.

And there's the town and the church and the school for all the regular social routines. And there's things that we do in the seasons – winter, summer, spring and fall. I suppose I could put all these images on a string.

These are all quite pleasant memories. But would they serve to make a book? Aren't they just stories that you tell as you watch old slides?

"The ship
is the most important element
in the voyage,"
thought the man on shore –
and the ship began to sink.

"We see, here, the soldiers wading through the rice paddies under cover of friendly fire. It can be very confusing to attempt to mount an offensive in a landscape that is so different from that at home. It is amazing that the spirit and resolve of the soldiers has remained so high."

First, let us look at the open truck, which we can think of as a space which must be filled. It has a cab and it has a dump-box. It has two high metal sides, one front metal wall, no tailgate on the back and, in a break in the side wall, it has a small door. The task, for the operator of the dump-box – the garbage-man who is dumping the trash – is to build a load of garbage, such as to keep the loose trash from falling out onto the street. It might seem odd to think of 'tradition' or of 'craftsmanship' or of 'legacy' when thinking of how to build a load in a garbage-truck, but perhaps a reader will concede that every human endeavour draws on a repository of accumulated lore.

How can we know the dancer from the dance.

My one-day taxi job. Driving a drunk down to Union. A couple of miles out of town. The dispatcher tells me he'll owe me two and a half. He stumbles out of the door and falls on the lawn. I get out and have a look and he's out like a light. How to get the two and a half? Can't be rifling through his pockets – calling softly but he's pretty-well gone. If I don't get the two and a half, I'll have to pay his fare myself. He could sleep here on the lawn all night long.

"Mary Park Passfield kept her experiences to herself."
"She never told her grandchildren any stories at all."

A mouse

A car which almost crashes into a truck.
A burst of spectacular fireworks in a park.
The satisfaction of a job well-done.

huddling snugly

Does Hamlet know himself?
At what depth is Hedda Gabler's deepest thought?
How can we know these characters who don't seem to know themselves?

in a nest.

Eight hours at the John Scott Tavern. Blackened timbers – splintered boards. A hundred and fifty years of debris. We leave the work-bull on the site so we can do the same tomorrow. The boss's son is driving the truck as we make our way to the dump at the end of the day. The sweat still pours down me as I sit and catch my breath. He glances at my work-shirt – wringing wet. Like to see a fellow sweat! Like to see him workin' hard! Only way to know we're gettin' our money's worth! I stare straight ahead – I don't say a word. I should have quit – I should quit now. But I won't – no I won't. We'll both be back at the John Scott Tavern the very next day.
Absent thee from felicity awhile.
Stopping off at a store near the Armouries. When I used to walk home after work. Buying a pint of chocolate milk – better than nectar to slake a thirst. Between the Armouries and the arena. Through the gully behind our house. Taking swigs of chocolate milk as I make my way home.

Chapter 9

Sometimes Herm is a little hard on the old truck. You'd think an old fellow would take it easy on another old one. Herm's legs are short and if he gets too far back on the seat, he can burn the clutch. He doesn't mean to, but he just can't push the clutch-pedal all the way down. Every once in a while I cringe, but I don't say anything. Fivey probably doesn't hear it – Fivey's off in a world of his own. Herm probably doesn't hear the squealing either, so the only one who worries about burning out the clutch is me.

I fled him down the nights and down the days.

My dad teaching me how to sharpen a hand-saw. Trying to hide the fact that I just don't care to know. They have power-tools now. No more need to do it yourself. I'll buy a power-saw and get someone to sharpen the blade.

To be a young man

A man and a woman standing on a balcony.
Garbage trucks converging on a central spot.
A boy with a stab-wound in his heart.

who is about

So – an author writes a book?
That book is a portrait of the mind?
That book accesses depths which we seldom see?

to get married.

A group of men holding a picture window.
A parade on Talbot Street on Centennial Day.
Kids running races at a picnic.

Old soldiers never talk. Uncle Ken was five hours from the Germans, all the way across Europe, and he only spoke about it once or twice. He was that close to death for a couple of years. Uncle Ken will never talk – I know he won't. He will never write a book – I know he won't. It's just as if he never lived that life.

The best that is known and thought in the world.

Wuthering Heights – Wuthering Heights. Perhaps the book that has had the greatest impact on me. Two people who live life right up to the brim. Over the brim, I guess I would have to say. Where is the other half of my soul? a reader asks. Somewhere out there in the world – I know – but where? I didn't know that a book could be written like that. The book is as pure – in my mind – as the icy stream that flows by Wuthering Heights. I wonder if the kids will spoil it for me.

Well what do you know – he made the team. He could skate with the greatest stars. Grab the puck and stick-handle through the whole team. He had a blazing slap-shot that put the goalies in hand-cuffs. The goalies would tremble every time he stepped on the ice.

"Perhaps the most controversial public person to come out of St. Thomas was Mitch Hepburn, the boy from Yarmouth."

"Mitch was the boy who came out of nowhere and rose to the top."

I am sitting on some bleachers! I am sitting in a circus tent! I am the only one in the audience! The clowns and the bareback riders and the lions and the tigers are milling around! They seem to be waiting for the ring-master to arrive!

Make it back to the shore - the men who were singing - I got to thinking - what is meant by - what is he trying to do - last and last for years - hasn't been a human story - would he be able to skate - all I could do - making life turn out.

Just a young Toronto boy.
Just in from the farm where he figured he didn't belong.
Got himself a job earning some money and flush with cash.

The jury
deliberated
for about a week.

Cutting the grass at the Old English Churchyard. Some of the graves are marked with wood. Some of the stone ones are chipped and worn. You can only read a few of the faded words. Just the names and the dates. Sometimes the age of a child who died. Sometimes a whole family lying side by side.

I'll lug the guts into the neighbour room.

Me on special pickup. Just me and an open truck. An old house. A lady has had the old kitchen torn out at the back. Old bricks with chunks of mortar. Some heavy stones and old two-by-fours –pioneer size – with old square pioneer nails. No driveway and no wheelbarrow, so I have to lug the refuse in arm-loads from the back of the house to the curb. What do I owe you, she asks. Three and a half hours, I think to myself. I get a dollar, twenty-five an hour. The boss has the cost of the truck and his profit. That was a lot of heavy work. I say ten dollars and she rolls her eyes to the sky. Halfway down to the dump, the boss waves me over. How much did you charge her? Ten dollars. Where is it now? I take the ten dollars out of my shirt-pocket and hand it to the boss. Three and a half hours and I had to carry it all to the curb. Did I over-charge the lady? Sounds like a lot of work – sounds fair to me. He tucks the ten into his shirt-pocket and drives away.

Or Olivier making all those Shakespeare films. Othello when he strikes his chest in anger. King Richard letting us in on his subtle game. Hamlet when he stands on the wind-swept battlements. I wish he hadn't worn that silly blond wig.

There's always one house with a double-double load.
Lydia Street - Glenwood Avenue - Ermatinger Street - Brock Street - Amelia Street.

I am sitting in the bleachers at the circus! The aerialists and the bareback riders and the animals are waiting to perform! A clown holds a whip in his hands! He motions for me to come forward! I get up and walk down to the ring and the clown puts the ring-master's whip in my hand!

Nurture these beans - the creek that feeds the pond - a massive monument - drop right off the edge - do all birds sing - everything the world does - I am not at home - fifty years from now - his ankles turned in - figure out a way.

Just a young Toronto boy.
Eighteen years old and whistling cheerfully as he works.
Tanned and fit and humming a tune as he hefts the cans.

He knew
that time
had gone forward
as the sun rose and set,

What did Grandpa Davies do at Gallipoli? Does he think about it at all? 'Churchill's folly' – 'the soft underbelly' – 'the Turkish guns'. He never mentions it to us and we know enough not to mention it to him. He fell into a history book and climbed back out again.

Forever wilt thou love and she be fair.

Heathcliff is a boy who is found in a slum and brought home. The old man who saved him has a daughter named Cathy. The two spend time together and fall in love. They escape from her brother's wrath and run free on the moor. Cathy is attacked by a dog and spends time in a nicer home. She becomes aware of the finer things in life. Love is everything to Heathcliff, but young Cathy wants something more. She is the love of his life and he knows it. He is the love of her life but she doesn't seem to know it at all.

A person who tries to flee from bad news.
A person who is too shy to get to know.
A wheelbarrow and a pitchfork at the curb.

So Shakespeare wrote poetic plays. For three hundred years afterwards, poets wrote poetic plays. You can travel the world and not find one on any stage.

She is wearing a dress of spangles.
It seems to be a faded green.
Some of the spangles are missing.
A broken strap is tied with a string.

A book is a dream?
A book is a nightmare?
A book is a dream-nightmare – a night-mare dream?

"The four Passfield-family grandparents died within the first hundred years of the life of this country, so they were not able to be at the cottage to celebrate with their children and grandchildren. Robert Edward Passfield died, relatively young, in a railway accident in 1917. His wife, Mary Park Passfield, died of old age in 1954. Walter Davies died, at age eighty-two, last year, in 1966. His wife, Eltrida Kennett Davies, died of breast cancer in 1950."

And what of a frog
croaking alone
on a lily-pad?

He wrote a humorous essay for his high school English teacher.

No hotel limo at Lake Louise Station. No limousine arrives at nine o'clock. I wait on the station platform until nine-thirty – and then quarter to ten. It's a pretty dark world out there. I decide that I am going to have to walk.

A father telling stories to his kids.

A librarian stamping a pile of books.
A family living at the Armouries.

I submit a poem to the student newspaper. Rhyming couplets in the style of Pope. Vignettes of campus life that I have observed. Too shy to talk to anyone – so I slip it in under the door. I read the newspaper for a year, but it never appears.

What goes up must come down – what goes down must come up. Writing is as easy as bouncing a rubber ball. For tragedy, you throw the ball up in the air – for comedy, you throw the ball at the ground.
Tradition and the individual talent.
Working with Frank on the stores. All the alleys behind the stores on Talbot Street. Once in a while, we move a car. The store clerks and owners sometimes park their cars in the alleys. They leave the keys in the cars so they can be moved. Sometimes they leave the windows open and if it rains, someone will roll the windows up. I get in and start the car. Classical music on the radio. I never touch any dials – I just drive. I pull her out of the alley and park in a two-hour zone. Then Frank backs into the alley and we load the garbage from the stores. Then Frank drives out on the street and I start the car and put it back in the alley again.

No, it wasn't easy being a garbage man. There was the time when they'd ended up with two open trucks at the end of the route. And they decided to back the one truck up to the back of the other one and combine the two small loads of garbage so only one truck would have to be emptied at the dump. And as Bud was backing the one truck up and he was waving Bud back towards the open back of the other truck, he'd panicked – as he realized that the two trucks were going to clang together – and he'd stuck his gloved hand between the backs of the two trucks to cushion the blow. And it didn't hurt his hand, but now his hand was stuck between the two backs of the trucks, so he'd had to call out to Bud, "Hey Bud! Move ahead a little bit!" so he could extricate his hand and get it free again.

I wasn't reading about what it was like to live where I was living – in St. Thomas, my home town.

I am standing in a circus tent! I am in the middle of the ring! I have a ringmaster's whip in my hand! I flick the whip and the circus performers and the animals all stop milling around! I crack the whip again and the music starts to play and the clowns and the aerialists and the animals all start to perform!

The treasures of someone's past - target-zero - hadn't know before - load every rift - a stack of old yellowed newspapers - still put quite a bit on her - the question was - the car shoots ahead - bring the two together - decision to just keep going.

Herm had been banned from driving because he had backed up at one of the schools and taken out the basketball stand.

And then, a little later that summer, Herm leaned over to pick up his first garbage can of the day, at eight o'clock one morning, and missed the handles and fell backwards and rolled right over on his back on the sidewalk like a helpless beetle.

And so what else was there to say when I'd helped Herm to his feet, but, "Hey Herm – looks like you're a little under the weather, so maybe this is one of those days when you'd better drive," and so I replaced Bumps in the back of the truck and Bumps replaced Herm on the sidewalk and old Herm took over the wheel, and did a pretty good job – inching one mile an hour from house to house – as the three of us – me and Bumps and Herm – took care of the garbage cans along the curb.

You will ride
the red river
into the chambers
of your heart.

An old mattress – stained and ugly. Try not to have any thoughts about that. Hard to find a place for a mattress on a truck. Lay it against the side and prop it with a hockey stick. Hope it holds and doesn't let the garbage leak out.
The deep truth is imageless.
So Heathcliff is poor and Cathy is unhappy at home. A man offers to marry her and take her to live in a mansion. She asks the old servant what she feels she should do. Cathy doesn't know her own mind. Heathcliff would never stoop to ask anyone for advice. He overhears the conversation. He overhears his Cathy say that it would degrade her to marry him. So Cathy marries another man and Heathcliff runs away. The rest of the story is much too painful to tell.

He would get a job holding the horses outside the theatre. The Shakespearean actors would be rehearsing inside the oval '0'. One day, he would mention an idea to Henslowe. An arm around his shoulder and invited inside. "Here's a quill pen and a flagon of ink – see what you can do."

It seems as if the garbage is easing off.
William Street - Wawa Street - St. Annes Place - Rosebery Place - Owaissa Street.

"John is cooperative and friendly, though very quiet and reserved. He is an excellent team member – though not a team leader – and works hard at hockey, where I would place him about the middle of the team. He is an excellent skater and handles the puck well, but finds that the pace of the game often puts a limit on his skills. He is very much a coach's player – always on time and very hard-working in the drills. He has not been scouted by any of the higher-level teams. I would not recommend him for higher-level play."

Missed the handles - your idea future is - my route all mapped out - looking a little unstable - just a nickname - pretty close to a void - carefully tearing at the envelope - waiting for the ring-master - a repository of lore - page stares back at me.

We went to pick up Herm one day. He lives at the Park House in this tiny little room. Barely the space to turn around inside the place.

A bed, a table, a chair and a mirror on the wall and nothing else. Not a picture or a calendar or a memento of any kind. The washroom was down the hall where the drinkers go.

Herm was flaked out on the bed. "Say Herm" – Bumps called out – "we're short a man on the truck – the boss said to come here and get you on the way to the streets." Herm opened his eyes and I wondered if he knew where he was.

Then he rolled over and sat up and rubbed his head. All he needed was his hat – it was lying on the bed. He had lain down drunk and slept the night in his clothes. Then he came out on the street and worked for eight hours.

"The ship
is the most
and the least
important element
in the voyage,"
thought the man on shore,

The typical garbage of the households of a town of this nature and size consists of brown paper shopping bags, cardboard boxes and garden-refuse, such as grass or chunks of turf. Occasionally, people discard an old bedstead or some boards. And then there is paper – plenty of paper – old newspapers and magazines. And occasionally, something exotic, like a lampshade or a broken easy-chair or cans of dried paint.

Ten thousand fleets sweep over thee in vain.

So my high school came to an end in five short years. My favourite teacher was, far and away, Mr. Prior. That was the year I came alive. Mr. Prior seemed to know what the books were all about. Told me to send my 'Splish Splash' essay to a magazine. Made me feel good even though they turned it down. I looked forward to university. My brother helped me map it out. No more Science and no more Math if I can help it. Put the lid on the Social Sciences as well. I'll take as many English courses as they'll let me take.

"Mitch Hepburn was a spellbinding orator, so they say, and was swept into office and then right out again."

"There's a story that would be treasured in any town."

A piece of paper

A boy who is scraped by a train.
A policeman waving a driver to come to a stop.
A bulldozer crushing everything in a dump.

thirsting

A book is the language in which we think at our deepest selves?
Made visible – in ink and paper – on a page?
A stimulus to consider – or let us say, to explore – the thoughts and emotions that are at the core of who we actually are?

for some ink.

Fivey is holding up well, as far as I can tell. Some of those cans have been pretty heavy. A couple of times I've jumped down to give him a hand. Don't know how much this job takes out of a guy with only one arm. And he isn't a kid any more. I used to dump myself into bed when I was fifteen and new on the job. Now, a half-days's work is almost a piece of cake – after my muscles get in shape when I first start out, that is. It's quite a stretch for him to reach, with just one arm and a hook. I'm leaning over and reaching down as far as I can.

Costing not less than everything.

Two people who belong together but circumstances get in their way. Their love is so powerful that it defies both death and time. We are made in heaven and thrust upon the earth. Our souls are made in two parts, but most people are never destined to know. The other half of your soul might spend its life on the other side of the earth. I can only assume that each soul is re-united after death. If Heathcliff and Cathy stay alive, they will never know. *Wuthering Heights* is the greatest love story of all time. It is easily the best book that I have read so far.

Chapter 10

We're nearing a very full load. I've been packing it in as closely as I can –
squashing everything down with heavier garbage. Hope we can make the rest
of the morning on just this load. In fact, if we go to the dump now, and the other trucks are near, we could be driving back up to the streets – with an empty
garbage truck – after they've gone. Might even meet them coming down as we
make our way back. They would wonder why we didn't stay and help.

Report my cause aright to the unsatisfied.

I loved university. Completely anonymous – completely unknown. I could
walk across the campus – thousands of students changing class – and not one
of them would know who I was. Just my brother and I driving to classes –
great discussions both ways in the car. Each of us taking our separate courses
– meeting for lunch downstairs at the lab. Spending my time in the college
library – thousands of books lining the walls. Reading all day and reading all
night. Every book seemed to lead to another. Hard to concentrate on the books
that were on the exams.

To be a man

Huge waves crashing against a little boy's chest.
A coffee table piled with magazines.
A father building a boy a wooden box.

who seeks to crush his enemies

So – why are you avoiding certain thoughts?
Thoughts of your grandparents – all of them dead?
Thoughts of your parents – now in their fifties?

like worms.

A student writing a humourous essay for school.
The Canadian flag flying over City Hall.

A fire raging in a garbage dump.

A writing assignment for Grade 13. An open-ended topic. A short story or an essay. We have studied both in class. In your handwriting, ladies and gentlemen, it should be at least a full page. Now don't write in large block letters – I know everybody's handwriting in the class.

That willing suspension of disbelief for the moment.

Virginia Woolf and her idea of tunneling behind the characters. *Mrs. Dalloway* and *To the Lighthouse* are the ones I've read. Telling the reader what the characters are thinking as they go about their day. I understand what the critics are saying about her novels. If only I didn't find her novels so hard to read.

Is this new kid a Canadien or a Leaf? Is he setting up Mahovlich or Richard? He could centre Frank Mahovlich and George Armstrong. Or they could move Red Kelly to the wing. Such a great young prospect – you can't leave him out of the lineup.

"Walter Davies returned to England and met his siblings and joined the Royal Marines."

"He met a girl from Faversham and they married and had five kids."

Why are you so head-strong, my girl? So young and so set in your ways. This young Montague is not worthy of you by half. You have conjured him out of your playroom. A rosy-cheeked toy from off the shelf. Once your father gets wind of your plans, he'll be put to route. You'll be sitting and watching the dancing – thirty or forty years from now – and all the ladies will chuckle and chortle at the foolishness of their youth. And you will shush all of the other fine ladies. And their eyes will grow wide with wonder as they blush at some of the stories that you will tell.

A highly-visual symbol - I make the rounds - you think for a while - little pebbles on the surface - then something turns up - the depths of self - one foot on the gravel - I don't yike fyoot - looks at me and shrugs - what is going on.

And what about Bumps?

What was he like in his younger days?

Are all of his fights recorded in the bundles of old yellowed newspapers that people tie with twine and put out at the curb?

That was the year
the jury awarded
a double-prize.

"Of course we all remember the President's press-conferences. He always seemed so sure of himself and in command. Always ready with a shrewd comment or a witty phrase."

Sunday School picnics at Pinafore Park. All the Anglican Churches in town. Losing myself in the crowd. Potato salad – hot dogs – ice cream. One of the ministers says a few words and then we eat.

Our little life is rounded with a sleep.

My job as a newspaper boy, during the winter. I bundle up, because it's bitterly cold at 5:30 a.m. It's quite dark out and the streetlights are dim. There's someone lurking in the entrance to the restaurant. How am I going to get my newspapers? Is it someone who wants to mug me? Will I have to fight him off? Does he think I carry money? What if he has a knife or a gun? I walk slowly towards the entrance. With all the clothes I'm wearing, I won't be able to run.

How did the actors get inside the words? The words that didn't always come alive for him. Many of the plays and poems had language that seemed to be old-fashioned. Some of the lines in the plays had corny rhymes. But those actors made those words come alive.

Wondering whether to take our second load to the dump.

Wellington Road - Station Street - Sinclair Avenue - Ross Street - Opechee Street.

I do not know how I know. I do not have to know how I know. I simply know. I would rather be a shepherd – or a cowherd – or a messenger boy. I would rather not know the things I have come to know. But when I am summoned to the palace, and charged with telling the truth, I have no choice but to do so. From whence does this wisdom come? – what do I offer as my proof? I cannot reply to such questions as these – I can only repeat the truth that I have come to know. I am not surprised when it is I who am then accused.

Be on the look-out - a barrel which is filled - invent a magic mixing-bowl - everything important anyway - try to hold it steady - at least twenty of his plays - a dusty old shed - under new management - I can build a wall - like signal-bonfires.

Did Bumps ever keep a scrapbook?

Did he show it to people in his prime?

And did he throw it into the fire when he came home to an empty room – broken and bruised – after the doctor told him that he'd just had his final fight?

while his life
had gone sideways
through the day.

Going to bed without an idea. This is Monday – the writing assignment is due on Friday. Tonight I worked on the two bears – Science and Math. It's going to be a busy week. I've got a Chemistry assignment. Mom will want me to cut the grass. Must be nice to be a writer and have nothing to do but write. How many great books were written by a student in Grade 13?

No man is an island, entire of itself.

Lying on the raft in Pinafore Pond. I shouldn't have let him talk me into swimming out here. It was a lot further than I thought that it would be. I don't know whether I can make it back to the shore. Will anyone save me if I start to drown? Lots of people lying on towels on the bank of the pond, but will they notice me or will I just sink down?

A queen cutting a gigantic birthday cake.
A nostalgic twenty-one year old boy.
A little boy helping his mom hoe weeds.

Why do some novels shine so brightly and some fade away? What is the difference between *Wuthering Heights* and *The Woman in White*? Does Science tell us that for every door there is a key?

She has a hole in one of her stockings.
Her shoes are faded and worn.
She is staring ahead at the spotlight.
Her lips are pinched and grim.

Thoughts of your brother and sister?
Thoughts of your relatives and friends?
People of flesh and blood in your daily life?

"As mentioned earlier, the Queen was in Ottawa and in attendance on Parliament Hill for the celebrations on this day – July the First, 1967. Every inch of Parliament Hill was packed as people stood shoulder to shoulder and sang *Oh Canada* at the tops of their lungs. The Mounties, in their bright red uniforms, were a highly-visual symbol of what our nation has come to mean on the world stage. Faces were beaming with pride and confidence as they sang *God Save the Queen*. Hundreds of coloured balloons were released and sailed up over the Peace Tower as Her Majesty cut the thirty-foot-high birthday cake."

And what if a camel
spits in your face? –
Is that a form of talk?

The teacher said that he should send it to *The Reader's Digest*.

Not a sliver of a moonbeam. No lights along the road. The night is completely black. I can't see the road beneath my shoes. I put my left foot on the gravel and my right foot on the pavement and I walk.

A family photographed at Pinafore Park.
A boy hefting hay-bales in a field.
The squealing of the clutch in a truck.

I share my thoughts with Bud, in the early days. "It's frustrating to think that somebody did a job a week, a month, a year ago, and yet I'm sent out to do the same job and expected to figure out how to do it all by myself." Bud empties a garbage can. "Well, John, I only know one big word, and it's got me outa more scrapes than all the four-letter words I've knew since I was a boy." He pauses and empties another can. "So – what's the word?" Another dramatic pause while he empties another can. "John – the ten-dollar word – the open-sesame word – is – 'improvise' ".

"There are times when reality and imagination seem to be separated by only a razor-thin membrane. To imagine a landing on the Moon is – now, in this summer of 1967 – not an image from the world of fantasy, nor a scene from a science-fiction movie. So close are we, ladies and gentlemen, that we will soon be able to see – before this decade is out, as President Kennedy promised – through the miracle of telecommunications – a human footprint on the moon."

People have a container in their kitchen. They put the paper shopping-bags in it and fill them with garbage. Then, when each bag is full, they put it in the garbage-can outside. Then on garbage day, they leave the garbage-can at the curb. So if they put the can out the night before, and it rains overnight, some of these cans have lids that leak, or some have no lids at all, and the can is full of water the very next day. Oh, you can tip the can and drain the water out, but the bags will be soaking wet, and the garbage will be wet and sleazy, and if you get enough of these, you'll be sloshing around in the back of the garbage truck.

A tattered coat upon a stick.

My one-day job selling tickets for service stations. Riding all the way back to St. Thomas in the back of the car. Chatham is hundreds of miles from St. Thomas on the 401. I didn't sell a thing. The others had a tough time selling, but most of them sold a few. Only one other boy and I didn't sell a thing. The clock glows on the dashboard. The day is getting dark. So if I'm working for a percentage – a percentage of the sales I make – and I haven't made any sales – that means I haven't earned a dime. I've travelled and worked for more than eight hours and I won't get a thing.

No it wasn't all that easy being a garbage man at all. He'd been asked if he would like to earn more money by going out to bring in hay after the garbage was all collected one day. Four more hours on top of the eight that he'd already worked in the hot sun. And he'd wiped his brow and stopped to sit on a bale of hay to catch his breath for a moment, while waiting for the truck to pull up beside him so he could throw on another bale of hay. And the boss's son had leaned out of the cab of the truck and said, "If you don't want to work, why don't you just go home?"

I read the novels and the plays and realized that they had meaning, but I had no idea what it was or what it might be.

I wonder if he's ever read a book. Not one of these, for sure. I keep taking them down and their pages are all uncut. Perhaps there is one thin dog-eared book beside his bed. Probably not – probably not. Some people are readers of books and some people are written by books. No doubt my mysterious host is one of the second kind. A very dangerous way to live, though he would never consider it so. His monogrammed shirts have already been worn by someone else.

Squashed and buried - a viable myth - something mysterious appears - emergencies out in the hall - a cold-storage locker - a thorn in the sandal - a great young prospect - bang on the side of the hopper - again he builds a wall - snow falling gently.

Bumps retired and then came back. Needed the money I would guess. Someone called him 'The Comeback Kid – more comebacks on the garbage than in the ring'.

Somebody said that he has a son. Nobody knows any more than that. Don't know how old he must be.

Old enough to get the pension? Why does Bumps keep coming back? Hate to think he needs this job to stay alive.

You will dissolve
and become
a chemical
in your brain.

Waking up with an idea. Some of the words are already crowding into my head. *"Since time began, poets have used seemingly unimportant subject material to make important and thought provoking comments about the societies in which they lived."* A mock essay on a popular song. An erudite analysis of the song – taking the imagery of the song to comic heights. As serious a poem – for our time – as an Ode by Keats. *"To prove our point let us pick a rock and roll song at random. 'Splish Splash' (words and music by Bobby Darin) comes to mind – a typical rock and roll song, a million seller in its day, a classic in ours."* Every line is a rift of gold in a block of ore.

Forever wilt thou love, and she be fair.

I love to read *The Waste Land*, but I have no idea what it means. I don't care what it means, I just love to read the words. The Queen on her splendid barge. The tramp steamer in the sweaty Thames. The space between the images. What do the two images – apart and together – mean to me?

He would renounce his aristocratic inheritance. He would write uplifting poems for the down and out. He would marry one girl and then fall in love with another. He would drown and his body wash up on a foreign shore. People would marvel that his heart could not be burned.

Wondering whether we can put all the rest on our second load.

Mabel Street - Glanworth Avenue - Edward Street - Devonshire Place - Burwell Road.

Uncle Ken has had a very interesting life – the first part anyway. We don't see him very often, even though he lives right across the field. He told my brother and me, one time, that he went all across Europe behind the D-Day invasion. France – Belgium – Holland – Germany. The Royal Canadian Electrical and Mechanical Engineers. They would fix any army vehicle that had its electrical system destroyed. They were right up close to the fighting-front and were told not to start to fix anything that might take more than five hours. More than once, he told us, he had to throw all his gear into the back of the truck and hightail it out of there. I wonder if Uncle Ken ever thinks about writing a book.

The pace of the game - drew on different muscles - not a hint - bubbling up from the ground - pay his fare myself - settled for something less - going to the sacrifice - nowhere to put it - a few of the faded words - standing out in the open.

Bumps and Herm and me were on an open truck one day, and a lady brought her garbage out to the curb. She had a lot of makeup on and she was obviously quite old. Bumps was up in the back of the truck and Herm handed him the can and the lady stood there and waited for the can.

"Say Herm," Bumps called out, "is it Hallowe'en?" The lady was standing on the sidewalk and I was sitting in the cab and there was no change in her facial expression. "Isn't it usually in October? – this is only the middle of July! – did they go and change the date of Hallowe'en?"

The lady waited until Herm handed her the can, and there was no change in her facial expression. She turned and walked up the sidewalk, holding the garbage can, and Herm walked to the next house and so I slowly moved the truck along the curb. I was in the cab and Bumps was up in the back of the truck so there was no way that I could see his face.

and the ship
sailed safely
to the shore.

"The official report on the progress of the war in Vietnam is very positive. It admits that there have been setbacks, but it points out the many localized instances that indicate that progress is being made. It also points out – however – that the public, here at home, should steel their resolution for the waging of a very difficult and protracted war."

So do we go to the dump and drop our load or keep on going? It's almost eleven-thirty – we're supposed to be done at noon. She's loaded to the gunwales, but we can always add more on top. Just have to build up the sides with bedsteads and the like. I'm thinking that we can make it if it hasn't been too heavy for the other trucks. Don't know how many trucks are on today. If the boss senses a heavy day, he sometimes makes up the crew for another truck. But if he doesn't, then we just have to soldier on. Herm and Fivey will do what I say – so I'd better make a decision. Do we take a trip to the dump or push on ahead?

The ways deep and the weather sharp.

My summer in the Militia. The St. Thomas Armouries. We sit outside, in a circle, in the shade of the trees, beside the parade-square. The Sergeant-major is giving a talk. The Sergeant-major is praising the best cadet in the squad. We've all been given an old bayonet and a piece of steel-wool. We have all cleaned our bayonets for half an hour. The best cadet's bayonet gleams like Excalibur. How did he get it to shine like that in half an hour? The Sergeant-major tells us we all should have done the same. A couple of guys away from me, there is a whisper. So low that the Sergeant-major can't hear. Wouldn't wanna stab an enemy with a rusty sword!

"Walter Davies served on the ships in the First World War."
"He served at Gallipoli but he never said a word."

A couple of beans

Old cottages with a widow's walk and a moat.
A lady dressed in spangles in the dark.
A boy who is considered to be an average student.

in the ground

Why think of characters in books of fictional stories?

Are they more real to you than the people in your life?
Is there a connection between the fictional and the real?

for twenty years.

Opening the mailbox and retrieving the mail. It just has to be published! the teacher said. This is the kind of humourous essay that *Reader's Digest* likes to print! My fingers tremble at the mailbox. What will I do if they turn it down? The teacher said that they would publish it for sure. The only time I have ever given one hundred percent! Carefully tearing at the envelope – they might have included a cheque inside. This could be the moment of the start of my writing career.

Whan that April with his showres soote.

Finding a rifle in the garbage. Enfield – 1861. With a stand on the bottom and a lightbulb on the top. Inside the barrel – a frayed electric cord. Asking around and finding out. Old, for sure, but not of value. The American Civil War. There are thousands of these old guns just gathering dust.

Chapter 11

The last few streets have been fairly light. Fairly light for the first day after a holiday. We'll lose a lot of time if we go to the dump. I make the decision to just keep going and call down to Fivey and Herm. I think we'll be all right. It's already eleven-thirty and we're supposed to be done at noon. Those other trucks will be closing in on us soon for sure. We can still put quite a bit on her if I start to build up the sides. There's an old bedstead and a few boards that I can use. Let's just keep going and I'm sure we'll be all right.

Time held me green and dying.

Asking the waiter for macaroni. Wondering why there's no macaroni on the menu. The other students look at me – who would want to eat macaroni when there's no need? I have always eaten at home – it's not student-food to me. My mom's macaroni has always been a treat.

To be a young man

A person asking how goes the battle, boys.
A friendly person waving to his friends.
A lady whose husband does not return.

who wants to be

How well do you know Herm?
How well do you know Bumps?
How well do you know Fivey – or Bud?

a writer.

A paperboy collecting money door-to-door.
Cars pouring out of the shops at quitting time.
Snow falling gently in the glow of the street lights.

My dad reading Churchill's history of the Second World War. Sitting and reading in the evenings while the rest of us watch TV. We don't ask what he's thinking and he doesn't say. He knew people from St. Thomas who died in some of those battles. He was stuck here on the railway and wanted to go. Everybody older than me has lived through at least one world war.

In the destructive element immerse.

Oedipus the King. An amazing piece of writing. Written in Ancient Greek. Thousands of years ago and thousands of miles from here. It says everything that there is to say about life as we are living it. But it says it as a series of questions. Is it the gods? – is it society? – is it the self? Human error? – simple bad luck? – some galactic design? What is making life turn out the way it does?

Is this new kid a Leaf or a Canadien? Is he setting up the old Rocket? – the Rocket's aging, but he can still put the puck in the net. He'd be perfect on a line with the Rocket and Henri Richard. He could play left wing if Henri didn't want to move. Such a great young prospect – some day you'll see his name on the Stanley Cup.

"The Armories is one of the oldest historical buildings in St. Thomas."
"Soldiers went out from St. Thomas to fight in all the wars."

I am enjoying the scene from my balcony! My balcony is one hundred stories in the air! From here I can see the landscape for miles around! But I cannot see the stories below me! It is as if my balcony is floating on a cloud!

The night is completely black - a bridge over a moat - figured out where i was - spends his life behind the curtain - the page is completely blank - splintered packing-crates - the obvious answer is - i am enjoying the view - she ain't so bad today - she has the idea.

But how can we know what a person is thinking?
How can we know what is going on in a person's head?
What was Bud thinking the day he took me by surprise?

In the early days
the sun circled
around the earth.

So – how to build a load on top of a load? How to build a load with no sides above the sides – with nothing but air to hold the garbage on the truck? How to build a load with no framework – no container – no vessel – no walls? How to hold water from the well when you have no bucket? How to hold water in your hands when you have no hands? How to make something when you seem to have nothing at all?

Roll on, thou dark and deep blue ocean! – roll!

That job painting the rooms of a house. I'm stunned – my blood turns cold – why would he want me to be fired? He says you didn't do a thing while he was up here! But I was listening to instructions! – I always stop and listen when the boss is giving instructions! – the same as when you stop and listen to the teacher's instructions in school! I told him that, but he says he wants you fired! He says that all the time he was up here, you stood around and didn't do a thing!

How many years did he have to live? Forty, sixty, eighty or more? It was obvious that he should make a life for himself. Simply note his interests and talents. And then strike out on a path that would lead to his goal.

Deciding to stay up on the streets with our second load.
Barwick Street - Willow Street - Church Street - Eagle Street - Fingal Line.

I am enjoying the view from my balcony! I love to scan the landscape far and wide! I hear a noise out in the hallway! I leave my balcony and go to investigate the noise! A piece of paper has been slipped in under the door!

The contemporary version - rises up to the heavens - my eyes are exposed - the edge of the bridge - string all the days together - inside this skull - he had a major dilemma - you have a job to do - a straight and determined path - things that have some weight.

The old soldiers never talk about the war.
My Uncle Ken just told us one story and that is all.
About the five-hour rule as he made his way across Europe – and then no more.

Each time
he received
a promotion,

Trying not to think about teaching. At least the negative part. How I might be too nervous and shy to do a good job. Trying to think about the books and the conversations we'll have in class. Not talk about ourselves when we talk about life. Talk about the characters as if they are real. Talk about them as people we know. Not let on which ones are us and which are not.
Speak of me as I am; nothing extenuate.
Oedipus thinks he is the son of a king and a queen. He has a very prosperous life in Corinth. But one day, his peace of mind is shattered. He is told that he is not the couple's son. He goes to the oracle to ask about the matter. The oracle has something else to tell him. He will become a man who will murder his own father. He will become a man who will marry his own mother. Oedipus immediately leaves Corinth and takes to the road.

A person who remembers everything which is important.
Neighbourhood kids all envying a garbage man.
A family watching the eleven o'clock news.

All lives have a surface. All lives have their depths. Why do some writers fish on the surface while others go deep?

The music soars in the circus tent.
The spotlight moves from the ring.
It illuminates the lady.
Her face breaks into a smile.

How well do you know your parents?
How well did you know your grandfather – Walter Davies – while he was alive?
How well do you know Uncle Ken or Uncle Claude?

"The Passfield children's Uncle Claude has many friends and acquaintances. He is the sexton of two churches in St. Thomas and is a very affable fellow. But no doubt his many friends all spent this very special day with relatives, or perhaps at one of the innumerable public events. So the Passfield family – and their Uncle Claude – Claude Davies – spent the day at the cottage on their own. Uncle Claude has quite an extensive library at the cottage, so the youngest boy – John – spent a good part of the day reading a book."

How do snakes
communicate?
By the tone
of their hiss?

The Reader's Digest said that the essay wasn't for them.

The sweat is pouring off me. My feet are getting tired – it's all uphill. A noise! – somewhere in the distance! Was that the sound of a cougar-growl? Can a cougar smell human sweat from miles away?

A Royal Marine carrying all his gear.
A boy and his dog out for a walk.
Flower boxes on display in the market.

Blue and white dinnerware out at the curb. Set aside in a clean cardboard box. A couple of broken pieces, but mostly intact. I know exactly who this is for. I place the box on the seat of the truck.

There are those who live – and there are those who write. Those who live are too busy to write and those who write are too busy to live. Is that blood on your hands? – or is it ink?

Though I sang in my chains like the sea.

That time when I didn't get the job. Sitting in an inner-office in a factory in London. The man is taking time out from talking vacations to give me an interview. So – 'John' is it? – have a seat – this won't take long. So – what is your story? He sits and stares at me and I stare at him. What's my story? What does that mean? Is he asking me why I want a summer job? Or what sort of future do I see myself as establishing with his firm?

And there was another time when he'd been haying. And he'd had a load of hay-bales on an open truck that reached up to the sky. And he'd pulled into the driveway between the truck-garage and the barn. And he'd forgotten about the height of his load. And he'd ripped out all the electric wires that ran between the truck-garage and the barn – and he'd realized that if the load had caught fire, he'd have perished in a truck-load of burning hay.

And then I began to read some critics who taught me to read the plays and novels as if I – I, myself – had been born and was living inside these books.

I am eager to get back to my balcony! From there I can scan the landscape for miles around! I read the notice that has been slipped in under the door! 'In view of the fact that the ninety-nine stories of this tower are not currently occupied – we have arranged to have all ninety-nine stories torn down.'!

Climbed back out again - is there a god - read every book and author - cougars don't take no prisoners - too early to look back - an interest in the form - ignore the scratching - they keep the best - boss is giving instructions - what does that mean.

My grandpa – Walter Davies – and his story of the ice-bound ship.
And never another word about the war.
Gallipoli was brutal, but if Mom hadn't told me he was there, I would never know.

Put dirt
in the ground.

Two cans to a house seems to be about right. One for Saturday and one for today. A couple of bags in every can. Most people don't have much except kitchen waste. Here's a house where they've put the winter ashes out.

I fled him down the arches of the years.

Oedipus is walking along on a country road. He meets a man whose carriage blocks his way. There are words between two hot-headed individuals. Oedipus kills the man and then goes on his way. He comes to a town which is being tormented by a creature. Oedipus kills the creature, by answering a riddle, and saves the town. He marries the woman who is the widowed queen. Her husband has gone away and has not returned. Prosperity is visited on the land.

Perhaps he would write some plays in French. The kind that Molière used to write. The ones where the master isn't as wise as the lowly maid. The characters' lives would tangle in knots to great applause. The king would send soldiers to put everything right in the end.

Wondering whether I made a mistake about the second load.
Barwick Street - Willow Street - 3rd Avenue - College Street - Regent Street.

"John has exceptional writing skills. His imagination is second to none. He only displays this talent from time to time, as most of the course entails the academic study of the great books of our literary heritage, and John is about the middle of the class in his response to the academic, as opposed to the imaginative, aspects of the course. He is difficult to know, as he is so shy."

At our deepest selves - having me fill out a form - no one could understand - i should have quit - a song about a doll - people you know - waiting to perform - bring home loads of books - was warned about that - the silent one.

Bud grew philosophical one day.
"My brother didn't have to fight. He was on stores the whole damn war – slept in a warm bed every night – three square meals every day – didn't have to slog in the mud and the blood. Everything nice and new on the shelves. Just a clipboard and a pencil was all he ever had to lift – an' here I am walkin' along and liftin' these heavy cans. And last winter, I got frostbite in my toes. I used to wait at the mailbox for a letter from my brother every day. I was too young to join the army. I'm gettin' tired of collectin' garbage.
"Alls I can hope is that we'll have another war."

The kettle-drum
is sitting
idle.

The dump-box operator – the garbage-man in the back of the truck – takes the clean brown paper bags of garbage and makes a wall across the dump-box of the truck, just ahead of the little side-door. Each bag is like a brick, and he makes a row across the floor with the bottoms of the brown paper grocery bags facing him. This makes a barrier as clean and secure as any wall. Then, as each can is handed up, he has the option of extracting the bags or, if the can has loose garbage, he can dump it over the wall. In this way, the front of the dump-box is gradually filled.

Oh I was young and easy under the apple bows.

My one-day taxi job. Stuck in Union without my fare. My customer is as drunk as a man can be. Sleeping soundly while I wait to get my fare. A light goes on in the house as I step up onto the porch. His daughter comes out on the lawn. Dad! Dad! Dad! This man wants you to pay so he can go! She takes the money out of his pocket and gives me the fare. I help her carry him into the house and slump him down in a moth-eaten chair. I get in my taxi and drive back into town.

"Old soldiers are known for keeping tight-lipped about their experiences."
"Many St. Thomas soldiers' stories will never be known."

The sun

A boy collecting money for his newspaper route.
Dreams that buoy one up or drag one down.
Kids stealing clover from their grandmother's field.

at the horizon

Your brother and your sister?
Friends you've made in hockey or at school?
How well – John – do you feel you know yourself?

about to shine.

Bud and the Third World War. Don't know why that hit me so hard. Didn't ever expect to hear anyone hope for a war. Can't see Bud thrusting a bayonet into an enemy soldier. What makes him think he won't have to do it though? Will he smile as the Russian bombers drone over St. Thomas? What's the guarantee that he'll get a cushy job?

Your procedure will be mine.

For many years the city is prosperous. The people look on Oedipus as the perfect king. But then a plague begins to destroy the crops and the animals. The people ask the king to intervene. Oedipus sends for a wise old man to impart his wisdom. This old fellow claims that Oedipus is the cause of the plague. How could the perfect king be a danger to his people? Oedipus sends to hear what the oracle has to say. He is waiting for the messenger to arrive.

Chapter 12

Everything the world does produces garbage. Every time a house changes hands, we get a whole household-load of refuse out at the curb. Somebody once treasured each broken lamp and dusty curtain and faded dress. Every one of these was brand-new in its day. There's probably bundles of old letters buried in these bags and these boxes. All the heartache and the joy of someone who's recently died. All to be squashed by the bulldozer in the dump. All to be buried under the layers of someone else's trash.

Thoughts that do often lie too deep for tears.

Going to Toronto and meeting some friends for a reunion. Students who worked for the summer at Lake Louise. Let's order Chinese – what do you like? It's a whole new world to me. Admitting I've never tasted Chinese food in my life.

To be an actor

A little town in the sunshine.
A cattle auction at a large hotel.
A worker who is drenched by a fire hose.

who speaks great words

Why do you not want to talk about your upcoming marriage?
Why do you not want to talk about your new job as a teacher?
Do you expect me to believe that you don't think of them at all?

in measured tones.

A steam train hissing in the roundhouse.
A boy colouring a picture in Sunday School.
A girl driving a shiny blue sports car.

A little white Austin-Healey Sprite. A sports car for me to drive to university. A heart-broken student. You can't possibly know how it feels to have to sell this car! If I don't get eight hundred dollars, I'll have to quit school! If I don't sell it, I won't be able to pay my rent! He flinches in pain when I tell him the bad news. The mechanic says that it needs a lot of work. A sad smile when I give him six hundred dollars. The mechanic said to offer not more than four. In fact, the mechanic said that I shouldn't buy it at all.

She never told her love.

The Old English Church. Digging graves for Uncle Claude. Just my brother and I today. If we have a problem, our dad comes up and helps. You can see the big white monument from here. Seven family members died in just seven years.

It's the kid's first Stanley Cup. He's had a tremendous year. All his goals are the kind that lift the whole team. It's amazing how he handles the tremendous pressure. I just know this kid will score the winning goal.

"Gertrude Davies Passfield grew up in Ospringe, in Kent."
"Her mother picked hops in the fields while her dad was away at war."

I believe that I finally have Hedda trapped. I have waited a long time for this to be so. I used to watch her riding her horses – the finest lady on the finest horse, looking down at the lowly judge on his way to court. You are riding for a fall, my lady, I used to say to myself. Have you considered that you do not own the very horse on which you are riding so smug and so proud? Your father is aging and you have no inheritance – you will some day be out in the cold – a little parakeet chirping and shivering in the snow – looking up at the cold, cruel world and wondering who will come to your rescue. And I will still be the judge – but time will have passed – I will now be the judge on his way home from the court.

Realized that they had meaning - I open up the lid - what kind of future - just flare up somewhere else - it's a little too early - world of his own - gives him a glimpse - reach way down - like stripping the bones - trying not to think.

These guys I work with.
You never know what they are thinking.
You see them from the outside– as if they're in a novel or a play.

The earth
was as flat
as a dinner plate.

"No doubt this funeral procession will be etched in the memories of this entire generation. The lift that the President gave to people of all genders and races and creeds was perhaps a hall-mark of his presidency. To see such un-bridled optimism come to an end – so abruptly – is a shock from which it will be difficult for many to recover – to overcome."

Port Stanley in the off-season. A completely deserted town. The empty beach where people lie on a towel in the sun. Just the seagulls and the waves. Just my brother and sister and me. Driftwood on the shore that was part of a boat.

In the poor benefit of a bewildering minute.

All the men are on their lunch-hour. We get an hour for lunch and we're eating our sandwiches outside the truck-garage. The boss comes along and points to the four newest guys and says, Get in my truck. So we pile in the back of the pickup truck and the boss drives up the hill to where the carpenters are working on the boss's new house. The boss's wife is there and says hello. See that window over there, leaning against the side of the house? Lift her up and hold her up by that hole in the wall. My wife wants to see what she'll look like when she's in place. So the four of us grab the big window and grunt and heave it into place, and try to hold it steady while the boss's wife takes a look. Then, when the two of them have talked for a while – the boss and the boss's wife – he says, Okay, you guys, you can put the window down. Then we all pile in the back of the pickup truck and then we ride back down the hill. We arrive just in time to get in our garbage trucks and go up to the streets for the afternoon. We ate our sandwiches as the boss drove up the hill.

But he figured he had a major dilemma. It was a problem that didn't com-pute. He had his heroes of accomplishment. That should open a path for his life. But he wasn't like the people he most admired.

Loading a great big piece of battered plywood.
Maple Street - Jessie Street - Henry Street - East Street - Arthur Avenue.

I have a father who is a minion. I have a sister who is perched on a shelf. They can be bartered for in the market on any fine day. Oh how I longed to get away. Oh how I shall hate to have to return. Father's eyes were sad and weary. Sister's eyes were ripe for pain. Formality upon formality – farewell upon farewell. All the while, I couldn't wait to get away.

We was thinkin' - I already borrowed - old worn leather suitcases - the most interesting character - right out on the street - something went wrong - those writing-manuals - problem that didn't compute - how goes the battle - marking the hole with chalk.

But isn't it the same with Hamlet or Macbeth?
We see them from the outside – what they say and what they do.

But why is it that people say that they can tell what Hamlet is thinking, even though they can't see into his head?

he retained
the position
below.

My little white Austin Healey Sprite. On my way to St. Catherines to see my future wife. Easing my foot up on the gas as I round a turn. Suddenly! – the car shoots ahead! – I am heading for a truck! – I'll go underneath the trailer and be crushed to a pulp! – I wrench the wheel back to my own side of the road! The car slows down and comes to a stop! The motor is roaring like an airplane! – I sit stunned! – in a trance! – I'm still alive! Not another car on the highway! I am trembling as I clutch the steering-wheel! I finally realize that my foot is still on the gas, so I raise my foot and the roaring stops. What made the car leap ahead like that? – I'm thinking through a fog! I fiddle with the gearshift! – the damn transmission must have popped right out of gear!
What folly to be wise where wisdom is a loss.
Thomas Wolfe and his dithyrambs – what is he trying to do with those? Lyrical passages that don't seem to have anything to do with the plot. Why would he write those passages? Why put them in the book? Why would two things be in a novel that don't seem to connect?

A book which is not completely realistic.
A little girl who almost dies of scarlet fever.
A garbage man whose clothes are pressed and clean.

Howarth – Yorkshire – England. St. Thomas – Ontario – Canada. Does it matter where a writer happens to live?

She rises up on tiptoes.
She moves towards the ring.
She raises her arms in acknowledgment.
The crowd breaks into applause.

Why the narrowing of your thoughts to just a few subjects?
Books and garbage – garbage and books – and nothing else?
Wasn't the Centennial of your country – 100 amazing years – just a few days ago?

"The culmination of the Centennial Celebration in St. Thomas was held at Pinafore Park. That's where all the Sunday School and company picnics are always held. There was food and drink and games all through the morning and the afternoon, as people strolled and basked in the summer sun. In the evening, some speeches were given and the pavilions had dancing bands. The late-night fireworks were mirrored in the waters of Pinafore Pond."

How would a mongoose
serenade
another mongoose?

He graduated from high school and went to university.

I walk with one foot on the gravel and one foot on the pavement. I hear noises – all kinds of noises – the whole mountain seems alive. There's a cougar in the area. I was told not to walk alone. I'm covered in sweat as I walk and walk and walk.

A fleet of fishing boats tied up at a dock.
A newspaper being tossed on a porch.
A family of five seated around a table.

A whole truck-load of books. Discards from the Elgin Public Library shelves. The librarian tells me that no one reads them anymore. Hoping no one will see me. I drive the garbage truck to my mom and dad's house. I back up to the garage and I unload.

"We do not know what words will be spoken on the occasion of the first human footprints on the Moon. What words could possibly rise to the level of momentousness of that soon to be epoch-making occasion? What words would you suggest, ladies and gentlemen, to be spoken at that awe-inspiring moment – as a summary of the thoughts of all humankind?"

Does the writer make the book? – or does the book make the writer? Do the words make the form? – or does the form make the words? Is a book made of paper or of ink?
Two roads diverged in a yellow wood.
Harold asks the guys a question. In the truck-yard, eating our lunch. He's been off for two weeks with an operation. It's a scheme that he has – to try to pay some of the bills. So I'll ask the boss if I can get my two weeks' vacation pay and not take no days off. Work right through my holidays and not take no days. So then he'd pay me two weeks for the vacation pay – that's my legal pay – and two weeks for the days I come in and work. So what do you guys think the boss'll say to that?

And there was the time when he'd been sent out to the new car-factory with an open truck. And been told to bring the discarded packing-crates – from the new machinery – to the dump. And he'd been told that all he'd have to do is to wait while the rubber-tired train brought the discarded packing-crates and the fork-lift raised them and dumped them into his truck. And then, when he got there – to the new car-factory – the rubber-tired train kept bringing cart-loads of packing-crates, but the fork-lift was busy somewhere else in the new car-factory. And so he'd spent the whole eight hours climbing down into rubber-tired cart after rubber-tired cart and heaving huge splintered packing-crates up and over the sides and into his truck, and then climbing down into his truck and trying to re-arrange the splintered crates so as to make a half-decent-sized load in the back of his truck, so he wouldn't have to take a half-load down to the dump.

But still, the books were all about people who were living in a different time from me and my family – and in a different place.

I only want what's mine. I only want what was taken from me in my youth. I have paid a heavy price. I am aware of it every minute I spend in the bank. Smug and comfortable – comfortable and smug, eh, Mr. Assistant Manager? You have no idea that I am a man who knows your wife. Hold your nose up in the air – look down on me and my kind. The time is coming when I shall put your nose out of joint.

A night-mare dream - perhaps they'll see it - hard to tell - I'd say we're okay - ophelia and the rest - insisted on that course - enter into your veins - the same hopes and fears - interests and talents - scan the landscape.

What is it, in the greatest books, that makes us think?
How do the greatest books differ from the lesser books?
How do the greatest books suggest the life inside?

*Put water
in the sea.*

Our little white Austin Healey Sprite. My future wife and I. Heading to the Shaw Festival – to see a play. Just a couple of hours along the lake. We come to a dip in the road – a slight dip for a railway track. I put my foot on the brake – lightly – and the car shoots ahead! My foot on the brake goes down flat on the floor! – if there had been a train on that track, we would have been dead for sure! Your brake-line snapped in half! the mechanic says. It was rotted clean away! I'd say this is more like a death-trap than a car!
Pig's head on a stick.
Being stopped by the police. I am driving my brother's car to get some gas for the lawnmowers. I don't have my licence yet so I'm not supposed to drive. The policeman waving for me to stop. I am about to get arrested, but then he waves to a funeral procession instead. Now he's standing beside my car while

we wait for the cars with the waving black flags to pass.

Perhaps he could write a massive epic. *Paradise Lost* had already been done. But there would be plenty of other topics. The grand sweep of the human parade. He'd think of topics as he worked on the garbage truck.

Loading four extremely worn rubber tires.
Woodworth Crescent - 3rd Avenue - Balfour Street - Drake Street - Glenbanner Street.

My dad has done a lot of things in his fifty-eight years. He's done every kind of labouring job that there is. His mother was a widow with five kids during the Great Depression. We all sat down at the dining-room table one winter – Dad and Bob and Ann and me – and Dad read to us from the diary he kept out West. He told us stories as he inked the pencilled words. He was a hobo in British Columbia, a cowboy in Alberta and a farm hand in Saskatchewan. He worked on the railway during the war – making up trainloads for shipment overseas. They worked on twenty-four hour shifts. He used to sleep in the roundhouse and then get up and work. He built two houses, by himself, with his bare hands. Surely in all of that my dad could find a novel or two.

They will never know - unable to sense anything - wasn't really news - better than nectar - to tell my stories - making architectural drawings - i've been packing it - what does imagery add - doesn't seem to know - words by which to think.

So Shakespeare had all the talent. And he also had the technique. What is it about the plays that make us think?
What is it in the plays that tells us – not so much what the characters are thinking – we can never agree on that – but what the characters might be thinking?
What is it that gives us – not their thoughts – but what might be their thoughts? What is the secret of the greatest novels and plays?

The fiddle
lies
beside the bow.

"Behind me, here, some peasants are being questioned as to what they know of the movements of the enemy in the area. Of course, not all of the peasants are convinced that a democratic government in Vietnam will provide a better life for them after the war. The difficulty, for the interrogators, is in determining just how reliable is the information that these inscrutable non-combatants tend to provide."

Once in a while, a cardboard box. Some are empty and some are full. The operator of the dump-box puts garbage with weight in box after box, and wedges them across the back of the truck. Again, he builds a wall – a wall of cardboard boxes across the back – a wall that is strong enough to keep the garbage from spilling out onto the street. When the front of the truck is full, he builds another paper-bag wall from front to back – from the paper-bag partition-wall to the boxes at the back – and dumps any loose garbage over that wall. Then he builds another wall – from the metal side-wall to the middle paper-bag wall – a short wall to keep the garbage from falling on his shoes as he stands at the door.

And miles to go before I sleep.

The two of us on a two-man truck. Bud is driving this load while I empty the cans and dump them in the bucket at the back of the truck. A whole whack of cans outside a restaurant, on the edge of town. A dozen cans, so Bud climbs down to help me load. I bend over and grab the lid and pull it off the first can and – my god! – the can is crawling with a thousand maggots! I step back with the lid in my hand! – I'm stunned! Then I turn the lid over and there's maggots wriggling on it too! I drop the lid and move back a step or two! Bud laughs and grabs a lid and his can is just the same! We lift them carefully – can by can by can – a dozen maggoty cans – and dump the maggoty garbage in the bucket at the back of the truck and raise the bucket up and dump it into the truck.

"She would go for walks with her siblings and their granddad, Henry Kennett.

"The kids would huddle in bed to the sound of the guns at war."

A flower

A performer barely seen in the dark.
A white-haired lady waving to her husband.
The assassination of John F. Kennedy.

about to burst

Is there something going on that you are aware of?
In a grotto now obscured by jungle growth?
In a cavern where a scuba diver can someday go?

into bloom.

My little white Austin Healey Sprite. I pause at a stop-sign near the university. A car pulls up beside me – the driver rolls down the window and calls. It's the starving student who sold me the little white car. He seems to have found himself a better set of wheels. Gee I really miss the old car! – this one I have now is just not the same! – it really broke my heart to see her go! All the time he talks, he is looking me in the eye. I'm just glad that she found a good home! Is everything okay? – is she treating you well? A car honks mildly and he waves and drives away.

In the hall the women come and go.

So that's the end of university for me. Received my diploma a month ago. Wanted to get out and get married and get on with life. Want to take lots of courses at night school. Just the ones I want to take. Want to read every book and author that takes my eye. Should be interesting teaching high school. I don't think I'll be too shy. Thirty people talking of books as the stories of our lives. But never talking about ourselves – the self is the life that remains inside. Talking of Hamlet and Meursault and Nora and Biff and Ophelia and all the rest. These are people whose lives we can live along with our own. These are the people who take us deeper inside our own minds.

Chapter 13

A couple of cedar fence-posts. Hey Fivey! – hand those fence-posts up first! Why would anyone throw them away? Cedar fence-posts never rot. They last and last for years. They'll be squashed down in the garbage and buried in the dump. Maybe someone will dig them up in a thousand years. Anyway – they're coming in handy as I build my load. If I get an old bedstead, or a big piece of cardboard – or maybe a chunk of old beat-up plywood – I can make a wall that will take a heavy load.

To err is human; to forgive divine.

I'm sure I'll miss the Oxford Book Shop. Used to go there on a Friday after classes at the university, on my way home. Every book I'd ever heard of on the shelves. And all in shiny, coloured paperbacks – just as if they were all brand-new. I used to park my little sports car and walk into the mall. On the way home from the agora in Athens – wonder what Sophocles has been up to lately? – oh here's the play that got such applause as he took his bows – a brand-new paperback of *Oedipus The King.* Wonder if Aeschylus ever comes into the store for a book-signing and a chat. I think it was Dante who was selling-and-signing here last week.

To be a young man

Two young men shovelling a load of grain.
A person who avoids certain thoughts.
A boy who drives illegally on the streets.

who is about to teach

Would you say that you are the greatest mystery that you are aware of?
The blank patches on the map that Conrad said he yearned to see?
The depths of self in which we are invited to immerse?

in a high school.

A lady who wears heavy makeup.
A bailer moving through a field of hay.
A monument to a family who died.

My first pay-cheque on the garbage. For every hour – a dollar five. Mom said, Put it in the bank. Your clothes, your books, your education. You're going to need every penny some day. My advice is to stay in school just as long as you can.

A feeling that I was not for that hour.

1984 is pretty grim. Don't know how the kids will take to it. I didn't read it in high school. University for me. *Animal Farm* might have been a better choice. Some of them might know a lot of history. Some of them might not. But then, again, you can see it as a novel about a couple of people. Two people trapped in a life-style and wondering how to get out.

Year after year in the chase for the Stanley Cup. Trying to win it for the fans. Testing his skills against Gordie Drillon and Mud Buneteau and Eddy Shore. Locking horns with Hap Day and Toe Blake and Gordie Howe. Always coming up big when the Cup was on the line.

"The newspaper in St. Thomas is currently the *Times-Journal.*"
"Once there were both the *Times* and the *Journal* serving the town."

I am looking at a page! The page is completely blank! The page is completely white! There is not a drop of ink on the page! I stare at the page and the page stares back at me!

Would be able to see - quite an extensive library - the nut is poised - take good care of itself - both dreams and nightmares - a portrait of the mind - welcome in every port - waves tumbling onto the beach - parallels and contrasts - if you don't answer.

There was a fire in the dump, and I was manning the fire hose, and Ivan, the bulldozer operator, was scooping up bucket-loads of dirt and dumping them on the fire.

We had the pump hooked up to the creek and were pumping water onto the fire, but the fire was burning deep down inside, so every time we soaked some garbage, and made the flames die down, more flames would just flare up somewhere else.

And someone shouted Ivan's name, and I turned with the fire hose, and there was Ivan on the bulldozer surrounded by flame.

If you sailed too far
you would drop

right off the edge.

No need to think about marriage. Coming up in a month and a half. Be nice to see Quebec City. Always wanted to see it some time. After that, the marriage will take good care of itself.

O dark dark dark – they all go into the dark.

My job as a newspaper boy, during the winter. It's the man who always wants his paper early. The man is lurking in the entrance with a scowl. We are there before the truck drops off the papers. I am bundled up and standing out in the open. He is under-dressed and shivering with the cold. Every once in a while, he glances at his watch. It is one of the coldest mornings of the winter. We stand and wait for the truck that brings the morning papers. We spend a long half an hour in the cold without a word.

So first he had to face one fact. That he was very, very shy. That he was painfully, painfully shy. In any group he would always be the silent one. He knew he could never get on stage and act in a play.

Loading a box of baby-clothes, neat and clean and tied with a ribbon.

Isabel Street - Jackson Street - Mariam Street - Naama Street - Victoria Street.

I have a barrel in my room! It is a very heavy barrel! I had to wrestle the barrel up the stairs! I barely managed to fit the barrel through the door! It is a barrel which is filled with gallons of ink!

There was ecstasy and there was agony - a book is a response - alls I need - a leap in the dark - the chains would jingle - trying to tell me something - my childhood ended that day - so what do you think - can't see into his head - stationed on the periphery.

And all Ivan did was move his arms and wave for water.

He didn't get up and jump to the ground and run away – he just sat there waving his arms and pointing at the flames.

So I played the hose on the bulldozer and tried to put out the fire, but the flames just kept leaping and wouldn't subside.

He was the dishwasher,
the cook,
the waiter
and the maître d'.

I know what England means to my mom. No idea what it means to my dad. He was born here and never visited there at all. My mom knows more of the history of his family than he knows or cares about. She would talk with his mom and his sister. He took a knife and cut the past away.

An order of ideas which are universal, certain, permanent.

A man named Winston Smith lives in a city in Oceania. Oceania is fighting a major war. Everybody is controlled by the ruling party. Big Brother watches everything they do. The party is teaching the people to speak a new language. There won't be any words by which to think. Winston is being watched by a camera in his room. Is there such a thing as freedom? He decides to keep a diary of his thoughts.

A girl who doesn't know her own mind.
A drunk man who is sleeping in his clothes.
A boy who wishes to be a classical actor.

Why do some Canadian writers move to England? Why do some Canadian writers stay at home? What – for each – would be the icing? – what the cake?

She rises up to the heavens.
To the top of the circus tent.
She flies though the air like a bird.
She lands with a softness that purrs.

The most interesting character in the most interesting drama?
Who walks around St. Thomas, day by day?
Who swims at Port Stanley in the summer – who skates on Pinafore Pond in the winter-time?

"In the evening, the Passfield family had a fire and roasted hotdogs on the beach at Port Stanley. Their Uncle Claude had collected driftwood in a pile. All up and down the water, there were fires on the beach as the other cottagers and their friends sat and talked. They heard a noise when it got dark – a loud bang, it sounded like – and they all looked towards the public beach. And there – bursting in the sky – was a huge display of Centennial fireworks. All of Canada was celebrating the momentous event."

I was actually
just thinking
of birds.
Do
all birds
sing?

He took every English course he was allowed to take.

Both of my feet are walking on pavement. I stop and inch myself back in the dark – I turn left and start to walk up the Lake Louise road. The climb is getting steeper and I'm soaking in gallons of sweat. The night is so dark that I can't even read my watch. Every once in a while, I hear a low cougar-growl.

A pile of magazines on a coffee table.
Two kids skating for miles and miles.
A wheelbarrow and a pitchfork at the curb.

I have a gun. My brother's bb gun. An older boy turns away and slaps his bum. He taunts me to shoot him. And so I do.

Most of these guys don't want to work in factories. There's plenty of work in factories – it's not the Great Depression – but they don't want to spend their lives inside. They want to be out and on the streets. Don't want the noise of the machines. Don't want a line-foreman breathing down their necks. Want to see what it is that they're doing. Sure a whole street of full cans – both sides – makes you wonder why you get out of bed in the morning, but a whole street of empty cans is something worthwhile. You can look back and see exactly what you've done.

Ripeness is all.

My one-day job selling tickets for service stations. I walk home under the streetlights and into the living room. Dad looks up from the newspaper. Mom comes out from the kitchen and says hello. We drove over and bought some gas – thought you could clean our windshield and check our oil. The attendant who pumped our gas said a whole bunch of you kids went off on a job. So what was the job? – how much did you make? – did you have a good day?

And there was the time when he'd been sent out to the roller-bearing factory and told to bring back a truckload of barrels of used oil and empty them in the dump. And the fork-lift kept loading the barrels of oil on the back of his truck until it was full. And when he'd asked the fork-lift driver why the barrels were so full, the fork-lift driver just shrugged. And when he asked whether they were going to put lids on the barrels of used oil, the fork-lift driver just shrugged. And so he'd driven as slowly as he could – about one mile an hour – from the factory to the dump, stopping every few truck-lengths to wait for the barrels of oil to stop sloshing and spilling oil out onto the street, and part-way down to the dump, the boss had driven up the street and stopped and told him that the secretary had been getting phone-calls complaining that one of our drivers was driving so fast that he was slopping oil all over the street.

And then one day, I looked in an old trunk in our attic and there was a daily newspaper – the *St. Thomas Times-Journal* – from a particular day during the

Second World War.

I move the barrel onto the table! The barrel starts to leak! The ink is black and flowing! Now my page is covered with ink! There is nothing but ink on my page!

A pretty dark world - can't wait to dive - shopping bag with a note - new avenues to explore - could see all the people - the nature of your dreams - great big tears in his eyes - something else to tell him - the most important element - tormented by a creature.

That dozer's filled with diesel fuel! – he'll go up like he's sitting on a bomb!

All Ivan was doing was waving his arms above the flames – just as if he was showing us where to dump a truck-load of garbage – but I knew why he didn't jump and run, so I just kept playing the water on the flames.

Finally, the flames died down, and Ivan backed the bulldozer up and away from the fire.

Put air
in the sky.

Boxes! – beautiful boxes! Sitting and waiting in front of a house! We can use them all for weight. Fivey tosses them and I catch them. I have them open on top of the load. I can fill each one with something heavy and wedge it snugly against the side. It will contain the lighter stuff as I build my load.

This is what I call living by ideas.

One day, Winston meets a girl. Her name is Julia and she despises the government laws. They meet in a room above a store. There's no camera or tele-screen in the room. Someone who opposes the ruling party wants to see him. This person is against the ways of the oppressive government. How did this person know that Winston feels the same? Winston and Julia read a book that exposes the fraud. There must be others in their society who think the same way.

He would write plays in which people chatted. Chatted of socially-advanced ideas. First the voice of the dull and the stodgy. Then he would upset the apple cart. Perhaps the Shaw Festival was looking for a batch of new plays.

Loading a set of golf clubs, with every club broken in half.

Hill Street - 4th Avenue - Ada Street - Mclachlin Place - Simcoe Street - Verna Street.

"John has been with us for a number of summers. He has done everything he's been asked to do. He started out walking behind a truck and emptying garbage cans. Over the years, he's done it all – this is a firm with many fingers in the pie. He has driven trucks, large and small, brought in hay, dug ditches, worked a fire-hose in the dump, and gets along with the public very well. John is a very, very hard worker. Ask him to do anything and he will do it well. I would recommend John for any job at all."

Why didn't they think - all of this is disturbing - these are the questions - a broken strap - looks at me and repeats - thirty or forty years from now - that world that simply is - you know nothing at all - plunge in the water - can look back and see.

I knew that Ivan was a hunchback and that he had a twisted spine – so I knew that he couldn't jump and run.

The hose was the only thing that could save him from the fire – he was simply playing the odds – it was the hose or nothing else.

I'd never seen a man so calm before.

The baton
is on
the lectern.

And now he fills the area near the door. This has been what one might call 'the garbage-man's office'. It's about the size of a phone booth – without a roof and surrounded by paper-bag walls. All this time, the garbage-man has been standing on the metal floor of the dump-box. His shoes and clothes have never touched the garbage. He wears gloves as he dumps each garbage pail. So now, he perches up on the garbage that is already present – making sure to keep himself high and dry. And he wedges boxes or old boards in the open space above the small door, and he fills his former office to the top of the sides.

A palace and a prison on each hand.

Grandpa Davies thinks it's amusing. I don't happen to think it is. I am complaining about the Militia. They lined us up for pay-drill and put our hundred dollars on the table. Then they kept a dollar-fifty for the regimental tie. They didn't ask if we wanted to buy one. I'm sure not going to wear a tie to school. He smiles and says, Welcome to the army. I say, I'm not in it any more. We handed in our uniforms before we got paid. A whole month for a hundred dollars and they make you buy a tie. My grandpa smacks his hand a few times on the arm of the rocking chair. I was going to ask him about living in the Armouries, but I get up and go. Maybe he'll tell me some other time when I stop after school.

"There are a lot of stories in those old St. Thomas newspapers."
"Hundreds of St. Thomas stories are waiting to be found."

A twig

Two people talking about their vacations.
A taxi driver who doesn't yike fyoot.
A boy who sells no tickets in a day.

determined to be

Who wonders – always wonders?
Why are we here and what does it mean?
Now skating on the surface – now diving down?

a mighty oak.

I wonder if this is the way through life. You work every day with people that you hardly get to know. Bud – Herm – Fivey – Bumps – and all those guys I've worked with before. You work with guys – you respect their privacy – you don't ask them about themselves and they never volunteer a word. And then when you try to think about them, what you have is pretty close to a void.

We are such stuff as dreams are made on.

One day the soldiers break in on Winston and Julia. They are put in prison and questioned for days and days. They ask Winston to tell the truth about Julia. They ask Julia to betray Winston as well. The two lovers resist and resist. Romeo and Juliet – Heathcliff and Cathy – Troilus and Criseyde. Then one day, the torturers strap a cage to Winston's face. Only one thing will allow you to keep these rats from eating your face, my dear Winston. Are you going to sacrifice Julia – or not?

Chapter 14

Oh no! A garbage can of loose paper. Someone must have cleaned out old wrappings that they kept from the gifts at Christmas time. This stuff is as light as a feather. Nowhere to put it except to spread it all over the top. Tempted to keep their can, but can't do that. Why didn't they think to tie it inside a box? This stuff is going to blow off the truck if I can't find something to weigh it down. But look! – what you wish for, Master, you shall have! A kindly genie has placed a tub of grass two houses away. I'll spread the grass across the paper to hold it down.

On evil days though fall'n, and evil tongues.

There was a person who came to our house who was quite surprised. He said that we all sit and read instead of talk. My dad reads books, my mom reads books, my brother reads books, my sister reads books and I read books. There's always a stack of magazines on the coffee table. We all go to the public library once a week. We kids all bring home loads of books from school. We read so we'll have something to say when we talk.

To be an old man

A conversation over brandy and cigars.
Whole boxes of clean magazines.
A mother analysing a humorous song.

who argues

So why the interest in the poetic drama?
What does imagery add to a book?
What does poetry do that prose cannot do as well?

with his son.

A mother telling stories of her childhood in the old country.
Two college students shovelling grain.

A young man making an architectural drawing.

Driving our little white sports-car to Toronto. The cattle auction at the Royal York Hotel. Interviews that might lead to a job. Last week, I went to one of the high schools. The Head of the English Department showed me around. Told me about his star English teacher. Declaiming Shakespeare while standing on his desk! You could hear him clear down to the office! He was Antony giving what-for to the Roman mob! I don't do good interviews. Too shy to shout at mobs. The interviewer was polite, but I knew he thought I couldn't control a class. I could tell by the way he said good-bye at the door. He made me wonder if I'll ever get a job.

And never lifted up a single stone.

Homer seems to do it all. He captures the rituals that all of us have in our daily lives. But he also writes about the great events, like war. Nobody here ever talks about the war – and we have had two – and some people think that a third is on the way. I know that – if I write – I won't write like Homer at all.

A long and distinguished career. The oldest player still playing the game. A little slower these days, but he's the wiliest veteran on the ice. Losing count of how many times he's had his name embossed on the Cup. Still the unassuming, natural gentleman he's always been.

"Cyril Passfield was working on the railway during the Great Depression."
"During those days, part-time work was all he could get."

Welcome Winston. Welcome Julia. Welcome to the world that the gods have wrought. The gods? – the gods are an obsolescent term. Welcome to the world that simply is. Do you think that the sun will shine some day? – that there will someday be a change? I have something I'm keeping in wait for you. A revelation for you, no doubt – a distracting diversion for me. I set a trap and then I find I have need of a mouse.

Instead of living your life - how am I to know - born inside the globe - no sound comes out - always walks with a limp - pointing at the flames - interested in words - as if he never lived - my heart is still thumping - ripped out all the electrical wires.

And there's a story about Fivey.
And this all happened before I came.
It happened when I was just a kid and riding my bike around the town – long before I ever became a garbage man.

Those were
good days

to be a writer.

"Interment will be at Arlington Cemetery. No need to remind everyone who is watching and listening of the President's exploits, during the war, on PT 109. We are told that his widow will light an eternal flame."

New marriage – new city – new job. Major changes in my life. Make good sense for us to get ourselves a different car. Never lived in an apartment. Going to seem quite different to me. Lots of changes going on when you get to my age. Lot of things to think about if I had the time.
True ease in writing comes from art, not chance.
That job painting the rooms of a house. I put my paint-brush down and wipe my hands with the cleaner. I say goodbye to Dennis and I leave the room. I go down the stairs – no sign of the man – and out the door. As I sit in my car, I fume at the injustice of it all. I've always been a good worker. I've worked hard at every job I've ever had. I've always stopped work and listened to instructions. The injustice is a stab wound in my heart.

He was a very private person who liked the arts. He was a private person who liked plays and poetry. A person who liked to sit in a room and read a book. A person who interacted with others quite awkwardly. A person who only felt that he was himself when he was alone.

Getting a little alarmed at the height of the load.
Loading an old mattress and a box-spring.
Baldwin Street - Aldborough Avenue - Celestine Street - East Avenue - Highbury Avenue.

So pleased to accept your money. Always find a use for a coin. I'll have the horse shod and ready in record time. Horses don't have cloven hooves. Can't say the same about men. The lady takes a drink and pulls the hood across her face. Think I don't know who she is? Think I don't know what you are? No doubt this lady will have some tales to tell.

Stood in the doorway - how these authors do it - for some reason unknown - so what was the job - this is a wonderful deal - why should anybody bother - how can this be - thinking through a fog - a long time to climb up the hill - depths of murky water.

Fivey, so they say, used to ride on the side of the truck.
The big truck had a massive hydraulic ram.
A ram that drove the garbage and squashed it against a steel wall.

In all those years

of steady progress,

Up and down the corridors. The cattle auction at the Royal York Hotel. Every want-to-be teacher in the province descends on Toronto. Every school board in the province takes a room. Sheets of paper taped on the walls in the corridors. 'Haldimand – 3 Math, 4 English, 3 Phys Ed. 4 French, 1 Music, 2 Cosmetology, 2 Shop.' Where's Haldimand?, I ask my wife-to-be. The hall is filled with busy shoppers. She comes back and reads the sign. Oh Haldimand – that's close to Hamilton – you could drive there in half an hour. It says they need four English – you should try that.

My throte is cut unto my nekke-bone.

A cup of coffee at Paul's Food Bar by the railway tracks. If you're professional, you get your coffee free. Police – Postman – Garbage Man. The only garbage men who come in here are the ones on the store-collection route. A cup of coffee costs a dime. Free coffee is the best thing about working the summer with Frank.

A boy waiting for a limousine in the dark.
A tired worker falling into bed.
A man who rolls over on his back.

What is meant by 'an objective correlative'? What is meant by 'delayed decoding'? What is meant by 'the preconscious mind'?

All the strength and power of the eagle.
All the coyness and charm of the dove.
She soars on wave after wave of applause.
She is entirely at home in the air.

And why do you read the thoughts of all these critics?
Are you not able to think for yourself?
Why do you wonder what others have thought about these books?

"It was a day of celebration. All contention and animosity were put aside for at least one day. The feeling in this land was one of harmony – for all and from everyone. Happy Birthday to all of Canada. We are so privileged to call Canada our home."

Do they sing
when they
are angry?
Do they sing
when they
are tired?

He read all of the books that interested him.

Finally, a light in the distance. Past Deer Lodge and on to Chateau Lake Louise. I climb the hill to the staff cabin and open the gardeners' door. The other three gardeners are asleep and I'm out of breath and my clothes are heavy with sweat.

A boy in the uniform of the Militia.
A figure-skater making patterns in the ice.
A group of kids lined up at a movie theatre.

A lady loses a twenty-dollar bill. I bend down to where it fell and pick it up. She thanks me and turns away. I knew her the moment I saw her. She would be surprised to know who I am.

"And – dare we do this? – suppose we cast our thoughts beyond the antici-pated first landing of humankind on the Moon. What is out there? What is out there, far beyond the Earth and its orbiting Moon – far beyond our Sun and our Galaxy – for humankind – adventurous, ever-striving, ambitious humankind – to encounter, to wonder at, and to explore?"

You place an inkwell on the desk. You dip the pen in the ink. Or perhaps you click the tip of a ballpoint pen. You place the pen on the paper. You look at the ceiling – or out the window – or you close your eyes. You think for a while. And then – you write.
Had we never loved sae blindly.
That time when I didn't get the job. Sitting in an inner-office – the inter-viewer and me. So – you've obviously filled out the application form. Have you checked off every box to the best of your ability? Too early to tell about hiring. Don't know yet how the summer will go. Just leave it there on the desk. The secretary will file it. If something comes up, we'll be sure to let you know. If you don't hear from us, then the obvious answer is 'no'.

And there was the time when he'd been sent with a truck-load of topsoil out to the new survey. And he'd been given the address and told to dump the load of topsoil in the back yard. And when he got there, there were loads of topsoil at the side of the house so he couldn't reach the backyard and there was a new driveway at another new house on the other side and so he had backed up on the new driveway next door and then cut between the neighbour's new garage and the house where he had been told to leave the load of topsoil in the back yard. And then, suddenly, the whole truck tipped sideways in some soft soil and threatened to crash through the wall of the house that had ordered the load of topsoil, and it was a new survey so he had to run from empty house to empty house to try to find someone who was home and living in a new house and had a phone. And the boss's son had come up with a jeep and hooked a chain on the bumper of the dump-truck and ground four deep holes in the asphalt of the next-door neighbour's new driveway and then when the big tow-truck had been called and solved the problem, they had cleaned up the load of topsoil and everyone had driven away and no one had left a note telling the owner of the house next door who was responsible for digging four big holes in the asphalt of his new driveway and whether anyone was going to pay to repair it or not.

And I realized that my own family had lived through the same experiences that everyone in the world had lived through, as they went about their daily lives.

My husband went away. One of those journeys that men will take. Time went by and he never came back and I was alone. There was a plague upon the land. I knew nothing of what to do. A fellow came and solved the riddle and killed the sphinx. I was replaceable, I knew. There was no doubt that he would be king. Not one person in the kingdom said one word.

Leave the windows open - standing on a rock - sitting on the bleachers - tell us what's going on - the man who invented - think about such things - I wish I had a voice - stumbles out the door - all lives have their depths - entails the academic study.

The big massive ram compressed the garbage under hydraulic pressure.

And Fivey used to hang onto the metal handle with one hand, and lean his elbow on the sill of the garbage-chamber door, as the truck drove along.

And Fivey didn't close the garbage-chamber door and step down onto the street and wait for the massive ram to operate as the manual said to do.

Put light
in the sun.

So tell me – 'John', is it? – as he glances at the sheet. These will be boys – no girls in these classes. They are what we call 'technical-boys'. They will be welders, carpenters, plumbers – the mechanical trades. They're not what you might call 'book-learners'. Oh they can read, but they have what you'd call 'a practical bent'. Stories have to make sense to them on the level of 'feet on the ground'. So tell me – John – yes, it is 'John'. I see you worked for a garbage company. So – did you work in the office – or did you work on a truck?

Simply the thing I am shall make me live.

F. Scott Fitzgerald and the image of the great green breast of the new world. He wrote a letter to Hemingway in which he told him what to do. Put an image at the end of a novel which turns a whole new spotlight on what the rest of the imagery in the novel just might mean. Hemingway didn't do what Fitzgerald suggested. Hemingway wrote 'bullshit' on the letter and filed it away.

Maybe a poem as raucous as Chaucer. Could he set it in his own hometown? Did Chaucer live in a magical kingdom? Or did he live an ordinary life? Hadn't he seen the Wife of Bath on the bus one day?

Having Herm drive out around a low-lying branch.
Loading some old hockey sticks that have worn out on the road.
Manor Road - King Street - Mcintyre Street - Laurier Road - Mitchell Street.

My mom tells us stories, but she never writes anything down. She tells us of the Guildhall in the market square in Faversham. And how the Davies kids would walk from village to village with their grandad, Henry Kennett. And how Henry Kennett went out to work on a neighbouring farm at twelve years old and his father made him the wooden box that we have in our bedroom. And how the family lived in the Miller's House in Ospringe, by the Roman Road. And how she trembled under the covers with the other kids, as the big guns boomed over the house while her dad was off fighting in the First World War. And how she couldn't go uptown here, in St. Thomas, during the Second World War, without meeting a woman who'd lost a husband or a son. I wonder if Mom has every thought about writing a book.

I could tell - a self-made zygote - leave the keys in the cars - we don't say much - offer as my proof - is no longer known - have need of a mouse - tends to play alone - whirl around in my mind - as if he was showing us.

And Fivey was waving to a friend with his free hand, and calling out – Hey Squirrelly! or Hey Knurley! or Hey Churley! or whatever he was calling – and the blade of the hydraulic ram caught his elbow inside the garbage-chamber and cleaved his arm clean off as Fivey shouted and screamed.
And there was blood all over the street, and someone came running and tied a tourniquet and the ambulance came and took Fivey on a stretcher to the hospital.
And that's why Fivey has only one arm, and finds it awkward to empty a garbage can to this day.

The score
has not received
one drop
of ink.

"Our coverage of the Vietnam War will continue in a moment. We will pause, now, to take a commercial break. After which, we will bring you the latest body-count."

And then, when the garbage reaches the top of the sides of the truck, you have a load. A load that packs on more garbage-per-square-inch than would be possible if you just dumped each can on the floor of the dump-box and let it sprawl. So, a few more cans of refuse, to finish the rest of a street, and you're off to the dump. And that's how you build a load in an open garbage truck.

I stood in Venice, on the Bridge of Sighs.

My one-day taxi job. The boss of the garbage company calls. You still interested in coming back? Couple of the guys we had here last summer didn't return. Turns out we can use you after all. Never did garbage smell so sweet. I thank him and tell him I'll be down at the yard first thing in the morning. I phone the taxi company and tell them I won't be coming in. Sorry to quit like this, but I found another job.

"Cyril Passfield went out West to work in the harvest and make a few dollars to help at home."

"Later on, he built two houses, with his father's carpentry tools, for his family to live in."

A pen

A person who lives mostly in his mind.
A row of dead moths on a window-sill.
The body-count every night on TV.

lying idle

So the greatest books have never been realistic?
So the greatest writers have all been pioneers?
What appeal does all of this have to the writer in you?

in a drawer.

Driving out to Haldimand County. Looking for my new school. The Cayuga Technical and Commercial High School. Built in 1962 – only five years old. It was a thrill to answer the phone. This makes for a legal contract, John. Binding for us and binding for you. Neither party can back out now that you have said 'yes'. Would you like to come out and have a look? You say you would be willing to supply. Next time a teacher is sick, we'll give you a call. The cafeteria meals here are nutritious. No need to bring a lunch. The cafeteria is largely student-staffed. It's a noble profession, John, when all is said and done. Here's to the beginning of a long and rewarding career. I turn my little white sports-car into the parking lot.

And calm of mind, all passion spent.

A whole truck-load full of boxes. All of the treasures of someone's past. What gems – what pearls – what diadems – are hidden under the cardboard and the tape? No time to look them over. No time to sort them out. Every one of them will be squashed and buried in the dump.

Chapter 15

I try to live without regrets. It's a vow I took one day a few years ago. Look back and learn from the past, but don't yearn for what didn't happen. Drive as if there's no rear-view mirror on the car. But my decision to stay up on the streets – I have to ask myself if that was a big mistake. I've built these sides as high as I can. I've propped up a mattress and a bedstead and a battered piece of plywood with some old hockey sticks and some cedar fence-posts holding them in place. I'm going to have to drive very carefully down to the dump. Just one jolt and the whole house of cards could come tumbling down. Unless I get more building materials, this truck is done.

Ah love, let us be true to one another.

It isn't books instead of life – it isn't books as an escape from life. I don't read a book as a mental holiday – I don't take time off from life to read a book. A book is a record of how we think our way through life. A book is a reflection of what it means to take a step. A book is a response to a gentle breeze or a tornado. A book is a record, in blood, of the path of a wounded snail. A book is the footsteps left in the sand by the people who have been here before us. All the agony and all the joy of what it means to be alive. The unsteady infant – the tottering old one – every adult and child in between. A record of all the tears and all the smiles. Oh – forget it – I don't know what a book is. I just don't know how these authors do it. But still, I think I have something I want to say. I just have to figure out what in the heck that is. All I can say now is – some day, I hope I get to write a book.

To be a king

A boy painting curlicues on a ceiling.
Kids shovelling snow on a pond.
A soldier cleaning a bayonet with steel-wool.

who is charged

What did that girl say when you were out at Lake Louise?

You remember the day you walked up to Lake Agnes Tea House?
And you agreed that Lake Agnes was beautiful in the extreme?

with causing a plague.

A tractor pulling a rubber-tired train.
An older man lighting brandy on a cake.
A group of kids singing a funny song.

The Red Cross Concert in our class. The Red Cross Concert every Friday.
My music teacher told my teacher that I would like to play. I sit at the piano
and say that I can't think of anything to play. She makes me sit for five whole
minutes. Then she tells me to take my seat. She has me sit at the piano every
Friday but I never play.
Tomorrow and tomorrow and tomorrow.
Gatsby will be everyone in the room. Though not everyone will know. Two
kids sitting and talking in the snow-white roadster. The green light shining at
the end of the dock. The foul dust floating in the wake of some very powerful
dreams. I won't talk about myself – they won't talk about themselves. We'll
talk of Tom and Nick and Gatsby and Daisy Faye. A skinny kid swimming out
to a ship in pursuit of a dream.

Sitting in pain on the end of the bench. Ferocious pain in his leg from that
tumble against the boards. It's broken – I know it's broken – but I'm not going
to tell the coach. When the coach nods, he limps out onto the ice. He snares
the puck and stick-handles through the whole team. A broken leg and still he
scores the winning goal!

"There hasn't been a human story that hasn't been lived right here in St.
Thomas."
"People here are as human as people anywhere else."

I am standing on a patch of sand! There is a stack of books on my head!
The books are very heavy! I am sinking in the sand! I am up to my eyes as I
sink in the sand!

He held himself up - turning on its axis - i was warned about that - breathe
some fresh air - out there in the world - a lot more of life - a low cougar-growl
- turn my face to the breeze - sit in a briefing room - put dirt in the ground.

There was a man whose name I don't know.
No one ever mentions his name.
And he and another guy went down to the hospital one day.

There hasn't been
a viable myth
since that time.

Should I laugh or should I cry? Every time we turn a corner – and find a whole new street of garbage cans – I feel as if the gods are out to get me. Then, just when I think we're loaded – not another can of garbage can fit on this truck – why then something turns up and I go on building the load. Grass to weigh down paper when I get a load of paper. An old shovel when I need a pole to shore up the sides. A couple of heavy boxes that I go down and help Fivey to heave, that I can set just in from the edges and pile the loose stuff up against. Is there a god of garbage-good and of garbage-bad?

Those dramatic moments when it reaches intensity.

Another special pickup. One where there wasn't any work. Just back up the truck and wait for it to be filled. They're cleaning out the old high school. St. Thomas Collegiate Institute. Where I spent both Grade 11 and Grade 12. The old radiators would spit hot water as you sat at your desk. Wrought-iron desks from the eighteen-nineties. Collector's items, you would think. Be glad to take one home and have it for myself. Too late when I hear about it – they've all been unloaded at the dump. Ivan crushed them all with the bulldozer. It wasn't my special pickup. I only hear about it later, when I'm talking to Bud.

He knew he wasn't a future Olivier. Nor a Burton nor a Thomas nor a Welles. Not a Brando, not a Dean, not a Clift. Somehow he'd have to spend his life behind the curtain. He knew he was never going to be an actor at all.

Wondering when we're going to meet the other trucks.
Loading a tub of left-over ashes from the winter-time.
Climbing down and helping to heft a can of slimy grass.
Centennial Road - Dunwich Drive - Ker Street - Massey Drive - Jonas Street.

I am standing on a pile of books! The books are on a patch of sand! The books are very heavy! The books are sinking down into the sand! I am buried to my knees in the patch of sand!

What was the role - taking our separate courses - one hand and one hook
- we find them anyway - you have conjured him - light out on my own - can't
think of anything - the container just dissolves - scored his share of goals -
don't seem to connect.

And they were there to clean out the ashes of the hopper of the hospital furnace.

And one of them went up top and one stayed down below.

And the one up top would lean over above the hopper and stab the ashes with a poker and get the ashes in the hopper to slide down.

he never had
a taste
of gourmet food.

Be nice to have a steady income. Oh I know there'll be expenses, but we both agree about money. Be nice not to have to rely on Mom and Dad. I'll be the last to leave – they'll be alone. Wonder how they'll feel about that? Take them back about twenty years. Perhaps they'll see it as a second honeymoon.
Til thy tears mixed with mine do overflow.
Jay Gatsby is born as Jimmy Gatz in the Mid-west. He finds that he is on the bottom side of society. His people have always had to grub a life from the soil. One day, he sees a yacht that is in danger. He swims out and his warning saves the boat. It gives him a glimpse of how the rich people live. There is mahogany on the walls and a liquor cabinet. And the captain is welcome in any port. So Jimmy changes his name because he wants to be someone else.

A boy delivering newspapers in the cold.
A student who enjoys reading critical commentary.
A story that is too painful to tell.

What in the world is 'umbrella imagery'? Can a soliloquy be written today? Is anyone able – today – to write a poetic play?

The music soars in the circus tent.
The lady descends to the ground.
The spotlight follows her to the bleachers.
She moves between the seats.

And you were walking down the path that led back to the Chateau?
And you were both first-year university students?
And you loosened up and talked of your hopes and your dreams?

"The Passfield family packed up their things in Port Stanley, and said goodbye to their Uncle Claude, and put their wet towels and bathing suits and picnic basket in the car. As they drove home, on the edge of St. Thomas, they could see the fireworks bursting in the sky over Pinafore Park. The whole family felt the excitement of the occasion – the anniversary of the day on which Canada became an independent nation. They arrived home late in the evening – just in time to watch the CBC evening news."

Do they sing

for themselves?
Do they sing
for others?

Biography and the poetic drama were his interests.

I peel off my sweat-soaked clothes and I run a cold bath. I lie there a long, long time, trying to cool off. The sweat is still pouring off me as I lie here in the tub. I towel off and get on my pajamas and slip into bed. My heart is still thumping as I wait to fall asleep.

A pile of debris in the backyard of a house.
A car in an alley behind a store.
People lying on towels on a beach.

'The water is cobbled with wind-ripples.' I write this on a brochure. I am looking out the window of the train. Someday, I'd like to be a writer. I am on my way to work at Lake Louise.

You open the case of the typewriter. Or perhaps you have covered it with a cloth. You check to see whether the ribbon is in need of changing. If so, you take a new ribbon out of the box and thread it onto the ribbon-reel. Then you click the reel in place and then you thread the ribbon through the mechanism and onto the receiving-reel. Then you place a piece of clean white paper in the typewriter and crank it so the paper is in position to soak up ink. And then – you look into your heart – and then you write.
Yes, of course, if it's fine tomorrow.
Two of us on a two-man truck. Out on the edge of town. One of the hottest days of the summer. The heat from the sun is pouring down. We're not allowed to open our shirts. All the houses are back from the road so we can't get a drink from a hose. No trees, as all the fields are planted with corn. But – the houses are far apart, so instead of walking from house to house, I jump on the running-board between stops and turn my face to the breeze. Roasting and sweating on the ground – cooling off on the running-board. Three more hours of this and I'll finally get to go home. Bet my mom is packing a supper. Can't wait to dive into the lake. This is sure to be a Port-Stanley night.

And then there was the time – early in his career – when he was the second-lowest man on the totem pole. And the lowest man was the young guy – a medical student – who had told the other men that he was going to be a doctor some day and so they had called him 'Young Doc' for the rest of the summer. And every day – for a week – Young Doc was sent to clean out a latrine. And every day the doc came back to the yard stinking of human waste and the question was – day after day for a week – as to whether the doc would quit or phone in sick some day and the second-lowest man on the totem pole would be called upon to go and take his place. And every day – for a week – to the credit of the medical profession – the doc showed up at the yard, with clean clothes and a smile, and was sent off to continue shovelling out the latrine.

So I keep brooding and thinking and brooding and thinking and wondering to myself – what is a story – and what does it do?

I am standing beside a pile of books! The books are as tall as am I! The books are very heavy! Neither of us is sinking down! The books and I are standing on a rock!

Try not to have any thoughts - I almost climbed - do all birds sing - alls I can hope - your skin will start to melt - how we respond - a cougar in the area - what's my story - didn't know the answers - will never be known.

And the man down below would shovel the ashes in the back of the truck – shovel the ashes so they would spread across the dump-box floor.

And when he'd cleared the hopper-spout, he would bang on the side of the hopper with his shovel, and that was the signal for the other man – the man who was stationed up top – to take the poker and send more ashes down the chute.

And the man down below banged and banged on the side of the hopper, but no more ashes came down the chute.

Put flesh –
put flesh –
on the bones.

Frank and the truck and the flower bed. Yes, he did drive the truck into the flower bed. No, it was not his fault. It was faulty steering on the truck. And when the mechanic found no fault with the steering, it was a case of a faulty mechanic as well.

The horror! the horror!

Then the war comes along and Gatsby becomes a soldier. He is stationed at a military camp to learn to fight. The young soldiers from the working class are invited to special events in the rich peoples' homes. Gatsby can't believe the sumptuousness of the dwellings. He thinks that a judge must be a multi-millionaire. The judge has a daughter whose name is Daisy. She wears white dresses and has a car that is painted white. Gatsby falls in love with the daughter of the judge. They promised to marry each other after the war.

He would wonder what he could write about. There were no novels or films about his country. The plays and poems always took place somewhere else. He had an interest in the form of the poetic play. But all the great ones were at least four hundred years old.

Looking down at Fivey way down on the curb.
Loading some legal papers all dumped loosely in a can.
Reaching down for a heavy box of *Life* and *Look.*
Wabun Street - St. Joseph Street - Rapelje Street - Penwarden Street - Nelson Street.

"A year ago, John applied to me to allow him to switch down from the four-year Honours English B.A. program to the three-year Pass English B.A. program. I understood that he wanted to get married, to get a job, and to continue his university education at night school; however, I tried to impress upon him that his education would suffer if he did so, as most people do not continue to apply themselves to academic study once they have undergone the distractions of the work-force. Despite my best advice, he insisted on that course and, although reluctantly, I signed a release-form and sent him on his way."

A stab-wound in my heart - last summer's guys - only a seer could solve - strange things happen - further than i thought - is it a curse - happened before I came - to live where i was living - not the original words - simply playing the odds.

And so he climbed up the metal ladder, to where the man was stationed on top, but when he got there, there was no one there at all.

And then he looked down into the hopper and there was a hand – just a hand – sticking out of the funnel with the ashes dribbling down.

And he tried as hard as he could to rescue the man.

You are an orchestra –
an orchestra
of one.

There is never any need to over-load the truck, as the size of the truck lends itself to four loads in an eight-hour day. When the truck is loaded – twice in the morning and twice in the afternoon – the truck is taken to the dump to deposit the load. And then the truck is empty and can be driven up to the streets to start the process – the building of a load of garbage – all over again.

A little learning is a dangerous thing.

I was thirteen years old. And it was the Fall of the year. All the new 1959 cars were in and a dealer was displaying them on the lot. And there was hot coffee and donuts for the people who came to see. And a boy named Robert – whom I had seen around town – was there, walking around and looking at the new cars, and he had great big tears in his eyes, though he never said a word. And his shirt was wet all down the back. And later – on the way home – one of the kids said that another boy – whom I'd also seen around town – had poured a cup of hot coffee down Robert's back.

"It's just a matter of time, I suppose, until these St. Thomas stories are told."
"All it would take is for someone to just sit down and write."

A duckling

A cougar prowling on a mountain-side.
A waiter who is disgusted with his clientele.
A person who likes the movies and the beach.

knocking his head

And she asked you what you would like to be in the future?
And you said – 'Either a writer or – maybe a teacher'?
And she said – 'You know what I think you'll be'?
And then she said – 'I think you'll be a teacher'?

against a shell.

Can't believe we haven't seen the other trucks. How much more garbage can there be? Did the other trucks go to the dump a second time? Did they all keep going with the idea that they would soon see us? Did they all decide to build a bigger load? Will we have to send one truck down to the dump to empty a load while a half a dozen of us wait on the street with a slew of full trucks until an empty one comes back? Why doesn't the boss or the boss's son come along and tell us what's going on?
They flatter, she says, to deceive me.
After the war, the girl is rich while Gatsby is poor. He finds that Daisy has married someone else. Gatsby manages to acquire a lot of money, in some mysterious way. He acquires a flashy roadster and a swimming pool and a river of monogrammed shirts. He lives in a mansion near her mansion across the bay. He stands and looks at the green light on her dock. He invites the girl and her husband to one of his extravaganzas. He wants to show her just how much he has acquired. He believes he can make their lives go back in time.
In the fall the war was always there, but we did not go to it anymore.
I am sitting on the back seat of the car. I hold a small football that my mom and my dad have bought for me. I wonder what is inside it – rubber or air? When no one is looking, I take the ice-pick from the kitchen drawer and I sit in a chair. I place the handle against my stomach and, with both hands, I pull the football against the tip of the ice-pick. To my surprise, the tip goes into the football and all the air goes out.

Chapter 16

Working our way along the streets. Fivey handing up can after can. He has to stretch and I have to lean over and reach way down. I remind Herm to be on the look-out for overhanging branches. This old truck isn't going to be able to take much more. There's gotta be other trucks a few streets away. Wonder how heavy it's been for the other trucks on their side. Still, we can't go down to the dump. We would lose the best part of an hour. It's way past quitting time and we must be near the end. So we'll just keep building the load and hope for relief.

Ply your book diligently, my boy.

Una Ellis-Fermor and the idea that the greatest plays were never realistic from beginning to end. Probably the most interesting critic I have come across. It was the poetry and the choruses that gave them their depth and their breadth – that made them intense boiling cauldrons of emotion and thought. So what is the contemporary version of those techniques?

To be a young man

Collecting garbage on the street.
John and Herm and Fivey.
Building a load in an open truck.

who is starting out

So what have these questions meant to you?
If you don't answer, then how am I to know?
Have you even bothered to listen while I have talked?

on the road of life.

Two kids skating for miles on a pond.
A boy and a girl and a little white sports car.
A shelf of new books in a store.

Bud comes walking around the corner. Looks like he's out for a Sunday stroll. He doesn't even look at me, way up on the load. Geez you guys – where you been? We been sluggin' away all mornin' all by ourselves. There's a truck just along the street back there and those guys can use your help. We was thinkin' you guys thought the holiday was today!

And gladly wolde he lerne and gladly teche.

There was war and there was peace. Global harmony and global unrest. Wedding baked meats and cold funeral furnishings. There was ecstasy and agony, in plenty, on the news. The world was turning on its axis – summer to winter and summer again. And the two of them had their hopes and their dreams.

Actually, his hockey days were over. He didn't play much anymore. Just a beer-league, once a week, with a bunch of the guys. He wasn't born to make the bigs. He knew that a hockey star was never in the cards.

"The Passfield family is a family of stories, like all the other families in the world."

"Most of those stories of the Passfield family are lost by now."

He looked
through the window
at the kitchen

Didn't have a licence - asking these questions - what do you know - I drew a line - chase the puck - is something worthwhile - giving an interview - the whole thing was spectacular - teach and read and think - I wait to get my fare.

I guess the whole thing comes down to a simple question. Does anything happen here – in St. Thomas – in Ontario – in Canada – that gives a writer something to write about? Why do other peoples write about their experiences and Canadians don't?

The little boy
stood
in the doorway.

Herm shuts her off at the curbside. Fivey stops handing up cans and talks to Bud. I work my way down off the truck. Picking my way among the debris. Stretching my one foot way down to the metal on the side of the truck. Then fishing to put my other foot on the little door on the side. Then I swing down and put my first foot on the axle and drop to the ground. The side of the truck towers up over me. She's leaning towards the curb. I've never seen a garbage truck loaded this high.

And ride in triumph through Persepolis.

Wolfgang Clemen and the idea that Shakespeare gradually developed his ideal technique. Probably the second most interesting critic I have come across. I took a pen and I listed all of all the Shakespeare plays. I drew a line across the page about half-way down. All of the plays that are most admired come after that line.

So what was the stage on which he could stand? What was the stage that would not be a stage? What was the public role that would not be a public role? How to interact with people without being in their presence at all? What was the role that he was born to play in this world?

Feeling relieved to see Bud out for a stroll.
Sunset Drive - Fairview Ave - Elm Street - Ross Street - Talbot Street.

He looked
through the window
at the trees.

Turning on its axis - inch myself back in the dark - a notice in the news-
paper - the glow of the street lights - basked in the summer sun - I like words
- bundles of yellowed newspapers - these are the questions - he snares the puck
- he just went on with life.

Do we meet Oedipus on the road to Port Stanley? Do we meet King Lear on the ice of Pinafore Pond? Is Hamlet called away from the University of Western Ontario by the death of his dad?

He couldn't
wait
to tell his mom.

I walk along the sidewalk – back behind the truck – and then I turn and look back up. Sure enough, I've built a tower – a tower of everybody's garbage – I managed to find a spot for everything that was left at the curb. I stand and marvel at the wonder. It is – it has to be – the perfect load.

In years that bring the philosophic mind.

It was just another day at the beach. A plunge in the water and a lazy after-noon on shore. Not everything was spoken. Each would gaze for a while out at sea. The world was turning on its axis – winter to summer and winter again. In their heads were all their hopes and their dreams.

A mother who tells a story of her childhood.
A dad who tells a story of the West.

A grandpa who tells one story of the War.
A grandmother who tells no story at all.

All of these thoughts whirl around in my mind. What is literature? – what is not? Easier to read a book than to write one any day.

Her makeup is caked and blurry.
The sweat runs down her face.
Her costume is patched and faded.
There is a grim look on her face.

Perhaps these questions are not for you?
Perhaps they were flies to swat or ignore?
Perhaps they have stimulated other questions that you might ask?

The lights are dim where I sit in the bleachers.
The lion-tamer, in the spotlight, works his magic.
The high-wire lady is gone.
At no time did she ever notice me.

"And that is the news for this evening. We feel proud and privileged to be invited into your home. Indeed, it has been a very special occasion. No doubt, this has been a very historic day. Thank you for tuning in to the CBC evening news."

Is the lack
of a voice-box
willed? –
or is it
visited
upon one?

He wanted to be a writer, but he didn't know what to write.

Is the lack
of a voice-box
a blessing? –
or is it
a curse?

My nerves are on high alert. I don't think I can calm down. My sweat is clammy as I lie here on the bed. I'm sure I heard the cougar growl a couple of times. I'll just lie here and try to think of something else.

A boy walking up a mountain in the dark.
An envelope with a ten dollar bill.
The smouldering remains of a fire.

These moments are the nectar. The hummingbird sips and flies away. Where did the hummingbird go? The flower is brimming with nectar. How soon will the hummingbird return?

Bud says he'll take our truck down to the dump. The boss's son took my truck down. You guys can join the other guys. That way we won't have a jamb-up at the dump. You guys can help to load the truck that's comin' along.
Water, water everywhere, nor any drop to drink.
And Moody L. Prior and the idea that the greatest poets failed when they wrote poetic plays. And whoever wrote about 'umbrella imagery', which is such an amazing idea. And 'delayed decoding' and all these other literary terms. I just keep reading and reading and reading. I just keep living my daily life. I have to figure out what all of this means to me.

No, it wouldn't be easy having a career as a garbage man. Actually though, he had only thought about it for a few moments at the end of one summer – when Frank had suggested it to him as they were on their way to the dump. He didn't say anything to Frank, but he decided that garbage-collecting didn't strike him as a good choice for a life-long career. Oh it had its rewards all right, and there were plenty of times when he'd felt the satisfaction that came to him at the end of a job well-done. But it was just as well that he was going to go back to school. After all, he'd already paid his tuition and he was well on his way to earning his B.A. And then he was going to look for a job that would match his education and his talents – so no, he didn't think he'd make the garbage his life-long career.

And what are the stories – I wonder – the stories that would link me and my family to every other person – past, present and future – in the world?

He looked
through the window
at the carpet on the floor.

Never stoop to ask - continue to apply - what, exactly, is a story - our pencils and our notebooks - a lady dressed in spangles - few writers seem to know - a clipboard and a pencil - looking for exceptional talent - it's a scheme - what's the guarantee.

My mother lived by the Roman Road in Ospringe, Kent, in Olde Enge-lond. Chaucer's pilgrims walked not a hundred yards from her house. Do pilgrims walk along Talbot Street in my home town?

That he had discovered
something
he hadn't known before.

The perfect load of garbage. The perfect load of garbage. Every wish I had was fulfilled. When I needed a box – I got a box. When I needed a fencepost – I got a fencepost. When I needed an old bedstead – I got one of those. Grass divots when I had loose paper and needed the weight. Everything I needed was always ready to hand.

Theirs not to reason why, theirs but to do and die.

Just two kids and a little white roadster. Talking about their hopes and their dreams. The world was turning on its axis – summer to winter and summer again. The future looked incredibly bright that day.

So what to write about, he would wonder. Thousands of years of wonderful literature. Was there anything left to write? What could he write that had never been written before? It looked like a long, long road and a steadily-rising hill. So – maybe he wouldn't be a writer after all.

Standing for a moment and thinking about the perfect load.
Gravel Road - Wilson Street - Southwick Street - Elmina Street - Oak Street.

He looked
through the window
at the sky.

Reads the sign - didn't want to know - without an idea - the outside of the globe - you'll be sloshing around - to seem quite different - if he had lived life differently - smouldering remains of a fire - cut the past away - you don't ask them.

Is it the eyes or is it the brain? What is the means by which we see? How do we see ourselves as worthy to write about?

That he could be
inside
and outside
at the same time.

I stand and watch as the perfect load is driven away. Nobody else bothers to look at it. Herm and Fivey walk away. Maybe they've seen a high load before. But it's the highest one that I've ever seen – and I built it all by my-self. Bud will back it up and dump it – and the bulldozer will squash it down. Maybe Ivan will stop the dozer and have a thought. Though maybe, if he wants to get home, he won't bother at all. How often do you reach perfection at any-thing in this life? It was the perfect load of garbage and now it's gone.

The falcon cannot hear the falconer.

Well – now that I think of it – perhaps there could be a follow-up article. Some readers might inquire – what do you do when the truck is full, and you have to stay up on the street and you have no more room? – what do you do when the garbage is heavy and you miscalculate the time and the size of the load? – when all the factors that you have mentioned are impossible to attain? But – on the other hand – that would ruin the whole concept. It would intro-duce a whole new topic. The article that I had in mind would only be meant to deal with the daily routine. After all, how often do circumstances force one to improvise what one would have to call – what I would guess I would have to call – 'an unexpected over-load'?

"Life was too busy for the Passfield family to sit and tell stories."
"It never occurred to them that anyone, in the future, would care to know."

A couple of beans

Four hours to do the route.
All the garbage must come off.
If there's overtime, you don't get paid at all.

in pocket and in soil

'The unexamined life is not worth living'?
A quotation that you have no doubt heard before?
Are some questions a thorn in the sandal on the road of life?

for fifty years.

At least an hour of overtime today and we won't get paid a dime – not even our regular hourly pay. Four hours pay for the half-day, no matter how long it takes us to clear the streets. I'd better catch up with the others. Hustle along and join them on the other truck. Wonder what's around the corner? Can't be too much garbage left. How do humans produce so much garbage? Don't they keep anything for themselves? Actually – I suppose they keep the best and throw everything else away. Well – I suppose we have no choice. What else is anybody going to do?

Caught and sang the sun in flight.

It'll be the middle of the afternoon by the time I get home. It's turning out to be a pretty warm day. It would be nice to spend the evening down at the beach. I bet Mom'll pack the picnic-hamper for when Dad gets home from work. We'll drive to Port Stanley and go in for a swim and then have some supper and then the others will sit around and enjoy the evening. I'll take a blanket and lie down on the sand and read a good book. Now – what great book am I going to choose as my personal feast?

Three Books

John Passfield: Saturday Morning– a novel
A twenty-one year old would-be writer, John Passfield, spends his last few months as a garbage-collector on the streets of his home town, St. Thomas, Ontario, Canada, in the summer of Canada's Centennial year, 1967. As he works, he compares the imagery of his own life so far – and of his upcoming marriage and pending career as a high school teacher – to the imagery of the great books that he is reading, all while in pursuit of building the perfect load of garbage.

The Making of John Passfield: Saturday Morning – a reflective journal
This journal records the author's reflections on the process of the crafting of the novel as it evolved through the stages of planning, writing, editing and polishing. It constitutes an effort to be as conscious as possible of the process whereby the single idea that suggested the topic of the novel was expanded into a complex work of art. Topics range from the nuts and bolts of novel-building to the nature of the novel as an art-form.

Planning John Passfield: Saturday Morning – a planning notebook
During the writing of the novel, the author kept a notebook which records the day-by-day development of the novel as it found its shape and style. The notebook reveals how a vast cluster of thoughts was sifted, selected, structured and polished into novel-form.

The Project
Together, this novel, journal and notebook comprise the twenty-sixth install-ment in an on-going novel-writing project in which the author is exploring the concept of form and meaning in the novel, and of the novel as a form of expression in the 21st Century. All of the published journals and notebooks are available for free download at www.johnpassfield.ca.

About the Author

John Passfield was born in St. Thomas, Ontario, Canada, and continues to reside in Southern Ontario, near Cayuga, with his family. He is interested in exploring the development of the novel as an art-form, and has written many novels, planning notebooks and journals in his search for a form for the poetic novel of our time.

Novels by John Passfield

Grave Song
The Agony of Robert Chisholm

Jumbo
P. T. Barnum's Greatest Creation

Pinafore Park
The Swan Boat Incident

Water Lane
The Pilgrimage of Christopher Marlowe

Rain of Fire
The Ordeal of Conductor Spettigue

Victoria Day
The Fabric of the Community

The Wright Brothers
Flight is Possible

Leni Riefenstahl
The Valley of the Shadow

Out of the Park
The Cogitations of Babe Ruth

Raskolnikov
Murder with an Axe

Death Day
The Apology of Sergei Eisenstein

Einstein
Wonder

Geoffrey Chaucer
Canterbury Bound

Ospringe
A Visit with Grandad

Pompeii
Vesuvius Dominus

Beethoven
The Ninth Immersion

Job
The Cornerstone of the Universe

Bethune
The Only Person Alive in the World

Terry Fox
Somewhere the Hurting Must Stop

Lord and Lady Macbeth
Full of Scorpions is My Mind

Cyril Passfield
Out West

Glenn Gould
Light and Dark

Emily Brontë
More Myself Than I

L. M. Montgomery
I Gave You Life

Pauline Johnson
Know Who I Am

John Passfield
Saturday Morning

Eleonora Duse
Let Me Have My Wings

See www.johnpassfield.ca for publishing information.

In Search of Form and Meaning:
Journals by John Passfield

Each journal is a day-by-day record of the complex process that a writer undergoes while crafting a work of art. It records the largest decisions, of structure and theme, and the smallest decisions, such as the choice of one word over another, and the constant interaction between the two. Each journal is a record of a writer's reflection on the craft of novel-writing.

The Making of Grave Song

The Making of Jumbo

The Making of Pinafore Park

The Making of Water Lane

The Making of Rain of Fire

The Making of Victoria Day

The Making of Flight is Possible

The Making of The Valley of the Shadow

The Making of Out of the Park

The Making of Murder with an Axe

The Making of Death Day

The Making of Wonder

The Making of Canterbury Bound

The Making of Ospringe

The Making of Vesuvius Dominus

The Making of The Ninth Immersion

The Making of The Cornerstone of the Universe

The Making of The Only Person Alive in the World

The Making of Somewhere the Hurting Must Stop

The Making of Full of Scorpions is My Mind

The Making of Out West

The Making of Glenn Gould: Light and Dark

The Making of Emily Brontë: More Myself Than I

The Making of L. M. Montgomery: I Gave You Life

The Making of Pauline Johnson: Know Who I Am

The Making of John Passfield: Saturday Morning

The Making of Eleonora Duse: Let Me Have My Wings

Available for free access at www.johnpassfield.ca.

The Novel as an Art-Form:
Planning Notebooks by John Passfield

Each planning notebook records the planning, writing, editing and polishing of each novel. Each notebook is an attempt to record, understand, and organize the vast cluster of thoughts which occur as one grapples with the various levels of organization which a clear yet complex work of art demands.

Planning Grave Song

Planning Jumbo

Planning Pinafore Park

Planning Water Lane

Planning Rain of Fire

Planning Victoria Day

Planning Flight is Possible

Planning The Valley of the Shadow

Planning Out of the Park

Planning Murder with an Axe

Planning Death Day

Planning Wonder

Planning Canterbury Bound

Planning Ospringe

Planning Vesuvius Dominus

Planning The Ninth Immersion

Planning The Cornerstone of the Universe

Planning The Only Person Alive in the World

Planning Somewhere the Hurting Must Stop

Planning Full of Scorpions is My Mind

Planning Out West

Planning Glenn Gould: Light and Dark

Planning Emily Brontë: More Myself Than I

Planning L. M. Montgomery: I Gave You Life

Planning Pauline Johnson: Know Who I Am

Planning John Passfield: Saturday Morning

Planning Eleonora Duse: Let Me Have My Wings

Available for free access at www.johnpassfield.ca.

Other Books
by John Passfield

Anthems I
Verses from the novels of
John Passfield

Oak Street
The Passfield Family

The Poetic Novel I
Influences and Elements

Intensities I
(1-100)
Verses on Various Topics

Intensities II
(101-200)

Available for free access at www.johnpassfield.ca.